Mum, Alzheimer's and Me: Staying Alive

Mum, Alzheimer's and Me: Staying Alive
is fiction inspired by real events.

Illustrated by Mary Redman
Cover design by Jane Anderson Design

Caroline Court
CARITAS COMMUNICATIONS

Mum, Alzheimer's and Me: Staying Alive

Caritas Communications • 5526 West Elmhurst Drive
Mequon, WI 53290-2010 • dgawlik@wi.rr.com

Printed and bound in the United States of America.

Caroline Court

Mum, Alzheimer's and Me: Staying Alive

ISBN 978-1-4276-2113-9

Fictional Memoir.

Caroline Court

For Mum

Table of Contents

Table of Contents

Mum, Alzheimer's and Me: Staying Alive

CONVERSATIONS IN LIEU OF AN INTRODUCTION

Neurologist's report: *Based on the relatively gradual, progressive nature of the complaints, the lack of other neurologic signs and the severity of memory impairment...This patient's dementia is likely Alzheimer's.*

Mother: "That sounds bad. I'm not dying, am I?"

Daughter: "No, you just have a bad memory."

Mother: "My memory is bad? My memory is *wicked*."

ৰ্জ ৰ্জ ৰ্জ ৰ্জ ৰ্জ ৰ্জ ৰ্জ ৰ্জ ৰ্জ ৰ্জ ৰ্জ ৰ্জ ৰ্জ ৰ্জ ৰ্জ ৰ্জ ৰ্জ ৰ্জ ৰ্জ ৰ্জ

Mother: "Can't I just go home?"

Daughter: "Where is home?"

Mother: "That's just it. I don't know."

Daughter: "We took you to the zoo yesterday, near where you used to live, and you had a great time."

Mother, *not recalling*: "You mean I was there?"

ৰ্জ ৰ্জ ৰ্জ ৰ্জ ৰ্জ ৰ্জ ৰ্জ ৰ্জ ৰ্জ ৰ্জ ৰ্জ ৰ্জ ৰ্জ ৰ্জ ৰ্জ ৰ্জ ৰ্জ ৰ্জ ৰ্জ ৰ্জ

Mother, *puzzled*: "Are we related?"

Daughter: "Yes."

Mother: "Are you my niece?"

Daughter: "No, I'm your daughter."

Mother: "What? Are you sure?"

Daughter: "Yes."

Mother: "So you're my daughter and I'm your mother. Well, is that ever nice!"

ৰ্জ ৰ্জ ৰ্জ ৰ্জ ৰ্জ ৰ্জ ৰ্জ ৰ্জ ৰ্জ ৰ্জ ৰ্জ ৰ্জ ৰ্জ ৰ্জ ৰ্জ ৰ্জ ৰ্জ ৰ্জ ৰ্জ ৰ্জ

CHAPTER ONE

Florida, 2001

The Other Side of the Door
by Billie

On 10/1/1, my sister and I peered through the screen, the portal of our 77-year-old mother's Florida condo. Unannounced and uninvited, we turned the knob of the unlocked door and entered her little shop of horrors. What we saw would reveal to us a boogeyman named Alzheimer's.

First, a foray into the kitchen uncovered a gallon jug of premixed Manhattans, two Kit Kat candy bars, a stale chocolate chip muffin, half of a banana and coffee. Practically empty refrigerator. No food staples meant no nutrition. What had she been living on?

We wandered into the living room, Mum there dressed in pajamas in the middle of the day, lying on her living room sofa under a thin blanket, eyes closed and hands folded over her chest. *Dead people in caskets look like that.* She smiled wanly as she opened her eyes and began to realize she was not alone.

We drifted dumbly into her bedroom and felt fear for her as we followed a trail of dried blood that began with the disheveled bed linens, continued on the floor's once white carpeting leading into the bathroom, and ended smeared on the toilet seat. She had been hemorrhaging from either the vagina or the rectum, and for how long we didn't know and she didn't know. And this was how, like the planes that pulverized the twin towers on 9/1/1, and at about the same time, Alzheimer's slammed into our lives.

Laxative tablets shouldn't have been in her possession, but there they were on her dresser. Her roommate and boyfriend Ian had assured us he'd remove or lock up all medication before he left on his trip to Scotland, and he may have. But upon questioning my sister's in-laws, whom he had assigned to take Mum on weekly trips to a grocery store, we realized no one had aided or monitored when she "shopped." She was on her own in the store. Who knows what she brought back with her.

But the horrors continued when the phone rang. It was "Sally." I identified myself as Joan's daughter. She identified herself as Ian's girl-friend.

"You're a friend of Ian's?"

"Oh, yes. I've been going with Ian for two years."

I felt afraid again for my mother. She and roommate Ian had almost married once. What had happened to that? Was it a sham all along? An arrangement? Ian lived with Mum. How could he and friend Sally not see her frailty?

"I wasn't aware that Ian had another girlfriend," I gulped. "I don't know if my mother knew that, either."

"Oh, your mother knows all about us. We take her around with us a lot. Last Christmas, we took her out to eat with us."

So my mother had this secret. How could this have happened? And how could I not have known how sick she was?

❧❧❧❧❧❧❧❧❧❧❧❧❧❧❧❧❧❧❧❧❧❧

Mum had never lived alone before my father died in 1990. If, after

2

his death, she felt lonely or anxious–and she did–she locked up the Florida condo, grabbed her car keys and a packed bag and drove to Wisconsin, alone. On the surface, that behavior looked independent and strong, but she was acting on impulse and those trips were geographic escapes from grieving. My doorbell might ring at 11 p.m. on a Monday or Tuesday night, could only be Mum. I'd open the door. All smiles, oblivious to the hour or the fact that I had to report to my school at 7 a.m. the next day, ready to teach, she'd cheer, "Let's have a drink and talk." So I'd make the brandy old fashioneds and she'd talk–lots. A drive from Florida, alone, allows plenty of time for unexpressed thoughts to grow.

She would route herself north via Atlanta and through Chicago, and rain, sleet or snow didn't stop her. So infamous was her link to bad weather, friends would ask, "Is your mother coming up?" knowing a yes answer pretty much guaranteed horrendous snow or rainstorms. After three days of visiting, Mum channeled her restless energy into the long drive back and the brief geographic escape refreshed her for the moment.

But in the years just before the Alzheimer's diagnosis, little fender bender accidents, including one with a state trooper, became too frequent. Ian, whose job required frequent travel, worried more about leaving her alone. She drove alone to Sarasota to spend Thanksgiving with a favorite relative, got confused, turned around, drove home and didn't call anyone. Not good signs.

Then this phone conversation in the spring of 2001:

"Billie, did I leave my suitcase there?"

"What suitcase, Mum?"

"You know, my black one. I can't find it so I thought maybe I just left it there."

"When?"

"Just now. Wasn't I just there?"

"No, Mum, you haven't been here in three months."

Silence. My stomach knotted. This was a heartburn night in the making.

"Well, maybe I was having a dream."

I hoped she was. That was me in denial.

Ian thought she was getting more forgetful. Prior to his leaving on a trip, he'd try to arrange for Mum to fly to Wisconsin for extended stays with me or I'd fly to Florida. That sufficed for a while; I had vacation time. But in September of 2001, he planned a trip to Scotland which would leave my mother alone in her condo for at least four weeks. Ian assured me and my sister that he had arranged for someone to administer her meds, take her shopping for groceries, and check in on her frequently while he and I would call her daily.

That arrangement did not work.

Ian called from Scotland; he said not to worry, "Your mother is all right." But each time I spoke with her, she sounded weaker. When my sister's father-in-law, who lived seven miles from my mother's condo, called to say Mum's electricity had been cut off because she hadn't paid her electric bills–the yellow flag on her electricity box outside–Anne and I hastily arranged emergency flights to Florida with a return ticket for Mum. We'd bring her back to Wisconsin and initiate appropriate medical intervention.

❦❦❦❦❦❦❦❦❦❦❦❦❦❦❦❦❦❦❦❦❦❦

On the flight down, I pictured Mum and Dad's four-unit condo development blended into a rural landscape that should have been called jungle glen. It included a large, shared outdoor pool surrounded by scrub palms, old oak trees, Spanish moss and climbing vines. I liked the muggy warm air and explosion of life in the middle of winter, even if some of the living were termites and snakes. The units were compact and attractive, two bedrooms and a bath and a half. Mum and Dad had one of the more desirable and sunny end units.

Impairment free in those days, Mum could rattle off the names of the area's seven converging rivers: the Salt, the Homossassa, the Withlacoochee, the Crystal, the Halls, the St. Martins and the Chassowitzka. I felt a sense of loss already, that visits to this Florida place of many rivers and warm memories would never be the same or never be at all.

One neighbor with whom Mum shared camaraderie was Jenny, a divorced woman who owned the other end unit. Jenny dated Ian who at that time owned and occupied one of the inner units. He was a sports writer from Glasgow, Scotland, here on a work visa. When he traveled, which was frequent, Jenny pretended not to be waiting for phone calls, tried to maintain her dignity when, as the lyrics to the country western tune go, *if the phone don't ring, it must be him.* After all, she had just bragged about how good he was in bed—she talked like that—and now he didn't call. It was important to Jenny to "save face" as Mum said. Mum and Dad and Ian and Jenny actually double dated, went out for fish fries, and enjoyed extended happy hours. The relationship between Ian and Jenny was on and off again, but the group always stayed friendly. After Dad died of a massive heart attack, people advised Mum not to make any big decisions or moves for at least six months or a year. So Mum stayed in Florida and leaned on her two friends Ian and Jenny.

At some point, Ian divorced his wife in Scotland, but I'm not sure when. Mum went over seas twice with Ian and even out to dinner with the ex. He also had a Scottish "friend" Fiona who came to the U.S. to visit Ian, and Fiona, Ian and my mother chummed around like a little family. I don't know how Ian explained these various women to Mum or how he explained Mum to them. I know Sally, the previously mentioned "friend," seemed convinced that Mum was "like a mother to him." Among an over age 60 group of unattached women, Ian apparently held considerable sway.

I didn't understand it, the Ian/Mum relationship, in those pre-Alzheimer's Florida days. My husband said they seemed more than just friends. In a bold moment, I gave voice to my questions, "Mum, are you and Ian romantic? I mean, is it boyfriend/girlfriend or just friends/roommates? What?"

Diplomatic by nature, British and jolly private, she replied, "I think it's a little bit of everything."

She'd have been giggling, too, if she could have read my mind just then—a childhood flashback, my fourth grade 4-H club days, raising checkered giant rabbits. My friend Lenore parked herself in front of my rabbit hutch to watch the drama of rabbits mating. The male rabbit mounted the female, bit her on the back of her neck and thumped around for a while, rather violently I thought. Lenore knew more than I did about such things; she was more advanced—had very big boobs already. She said the male rabbit puts his thing in her thing and that's how they mate, just like people.

"Like people?" I protested. My parents would never do something like that, I hoped.

She did not relent. "Ask your mother if you don't believe me."

So I asked Mum and braced for an expression of horror, of Lenore being summarily banned from the premises. Mum giggled and told me I would understand when I was older. That's how I learned Lenore's unfathomable thumping-among-humans theory was fact.

Mum had charming ways then and still does of skillfully deflecting questions. She laughed when other people laughed, smiled when she was supposed to, etc. The Alzheimer's didn't change her personality or her appearance so both helped conceal her deteriorating memory. That's how she kept her Alzheimer's a secret.

But she had created an isolated world for herself, and that really began when she fell in love with and married an American GI, my father, in 1945. At age 20, Mum immigrated to America and that meant leaving her whole family behind. When Dad died, none of his family lived in Florida. All of Mum's family, with the exception of a brother in Pennsylvania, lived in England and Scotland. Now her Florida world consisted of Ian and his friends. The two visited Ian's golf friends in Miami, she accompanied him on his road trips to golf tournaments in California and Arizona, and at some point he moved into her condo and bought another one to generate more income. Now he owned two of the Florida condos and Mum owned (held the mortgage on) a third. Jenny had relocated. It was a sweet arrangement at first. Mum had his company and his help, financial as well as emotional, I thought; he had rental income, her company, and discounted room and board, I suspected. Just before Thanksgiving of 1999, Ian announced they were to be married, news received with some skepticism because of Mum's advanced age and Ian's track record. The plan was a civil ceremony in a courthouse in Florida, just the two of them. Then they would fly to Wisconsin to celebrate Thanksgiving and their wedding with us.

On the appointed day, Mum decked herself out in a white suit with a very short, not age appropriate skirt—her image of herself never aged—but she did worry about how others would regard the age difference between them, she later confessed. She should have worried about the state of Florida's prerequisites for nuptials, among them a social security number. The clerk at the courthouse looked up the statutes and read them to Ian. Even glib, persuasive Ian had no effective defense. He was not a U.S. citizen and he needed a social security number.

The wedding didn't happen but the Thanksgiving visit did. I trespassed on private territory by asking Mum if she thought she and Ian would get married later and she said, "He hasn't mentioned it." I felt that I had pressed on a bruised spot. It was none of my business, so I never asked her again; she never brought it up and they never got married.

❦❦❦❦❦❦❦❦❦❦❦❦❦❦❦❦❦❦❦❦❦

In April of 2001, Ian began to wean Mum off of the anti-anxiety drug Ativan. She had a legitimate prescription, but Ian suspected it was a cause of her confusion, her dependency psychological only, so without the supervision of a doctor, he "dried her out." Mum shared none of this with me but Ian wrote:

This is not easy to write... I live in hope that Joan did not get like this in a day or two so maybe the mists will clear in a little while when the drugs are out of her system... She is now resting, perspiring (side effect) and pulled the shades to have the room darkened (another side effect).

In July of 2001, during one of Ian's absences, I flew to Tampa and rented a car for the drive to Mum's condo. Mum had not been feeling well, could be anxiety, maybe not. She had a long history of morning anxiety, accompanying nausea and trouble sleeping. I took her to a new doctor Ian located. He wanted no more of the doctor who pre-scribed Ativan. I mentioned her trouble with memory, and the doc-tor said sleep deprivation can cause memory decline, that memory needed to be jogged, but he didn't order an evaluation. The doctor prescribed a sleep medication.

As the events preceding her Alzheimer's diagnosis neared, we noticed, as did Ian, Mum's befuddlement with finances, distress over the cost of new dentures and a new car, etc. Where was she financially? Ian wrote:

She can't grasp things like my name is on her bank account—it's because she always gets lost over her account—and I find all sorts of disturbing stuff like an application for money on which she has written the tele number and "no money" so God knows what was going on there.

My husband, a certified public accountant, offered to oversee finances for her but she declined. "I'm doing all right," she said. So during my Florida visit, I took Mum with me to her bank, to see for myself what kind of financial mess she might be in. Ian had opened a joint account where Mum's social security and small pension were deposited. From that account her mortgage, utility bills and other expenses were paid. The bank took charge—for a fee—of paying her master card minimum each month. The clerk said the arrangement would work as long as there were no overdrafts. But the bank paid the minimum balance of $33 a month of a $3000 credit card bill, so that balance would never be paid off and Mum was losing money each month. Mum thought the lady was "nice," and she was glad it had all been set up for her. Mum had no knowledge of what investments she had, what her mortgage balance was, etc.

The paperwork trail suggested some borrowing against the equity in her condo. It didn't show any deposits other than Mum's social security and a small pension.

"Mum, does Ian split your monthly mortgage payment with you?"

"No."

"Did he ever?"

9

"No."

"Well, it seems like that would help. What would happen if you asked him?"

"I don't know."

"Are you afraid he would leave?"

"No, I just don't want to make waves right now. I probably should talk to him about it, but not now."

"What's wrong with now?"

"I'm sick."

"What do you mean sick?"

"I just don't feel right."

If she already was hemorrhaging, she wasn't telling me. If she was really not feeling well, I would not know if the feelings were anxiety or something physical because she wouldn't necessarily know herself. And then there is the possibility that she just did not want to confront Ian and being sick was an excuse.

When I suspected her lifestyle was beyond her capabilities (and I didn't even know then about Ian's other girlfriend Sally), I tried to entice her with the idea of returning to Wisconsin. But to her, that represented a loss of independence. "You've got family in Wisconsin," I said. Of her nine brother and sister-in-laws, only Lee in Hodag, Wisconsin, and Louis in California still survived, but Mum could go out to lunch with the rest of us, the locals, like in the old days, we told her. She didn't bite, told me she was "happy" in Florida and that she would let us know if she needed help. This was summer, my vacation ending soon.

"I have to go back to school at the end of August, "I reminded her. "Ian is going to Scotland sometime in September and you'll be alone here. What if you're sick?"

"I'll cross that bridge when I come to it." Mum admonished impatience when I was growing up. "The best comes to those who wait," she'd insist. The sentiment is also an excuse for inertia. She would just wait for a crisis.

Prior to leaving, Ian called Mum's clinic and described Mum's symptoms. "Are you family?" they asked. No he was not. They told him he would have to bring in the family for this one. He knew, of course, that might mean Mum going back to Wisconsin. And that bitter pill he and Mum were not prepared to swallow.

⋘⋘⋘⋘⋘⋘⋘⋘⋘⋘⋘⋘⋘⋘⋘⋘⋘⋘⋘⋘⋘⋘

Flash forward to my October 2001 conversation with Sally. I wanted to hang up but just couldn't end the conversation until all was revealed. I told her my sister Anne and I were taking Mum back to Wisconsin, that there was blood all over the place, she was so sick she could barely walk and appeared to have lost a lot of weight.

Sally said Ian and she both thought a great deal of Joan, that Ian had asked her to "check up" on Joan while he was gone and to help her pay her bills. "I asked her if she needed help with her bills, but she said no," Sally defended herself. "She seemed all right [People with an Alzheimer's afflicted loved one hate this ubiquitous comment]; I even took her out to lunch at Burger King. You know your mother doesn't need medical attention. What she really needs is a babysitter...."

Then Ian called from Scotland. Sally must have contacted him and told him that my sister and I were absconding with his Joan. I told him that a stack of bills—two months behind in payments—sat on her kitchen table, and her electricity had been turned off. I described the scene in the bedroom and questioned whether anyone had even been in the condo for days if not weeks. And I added," I didn't know you had another girl friend."

He denied that. Didn't know why Sally, just his "friend," said something like that.

Mum's feeble position was, "I don't care if there are other women as long as he takes care of me."

⊱⊰⊱⊰⊱⊰⊱⊰⊱⊰⊱⊰⊱⊰⊱⊰⊱⊰⊱⊰⊱⊰

After we moved Mum to Wisconsin, in October of 2001, I, as her power of attorney, tried to close Mum's joint bank account. First, I asked Ian to close it. He said he didn't want to "stand in line at the bank." He was feeling uncooperative, didn't like my blaming him for what happened to Mum, didn't like my making decisions for her without input from him. He did not believe she had Alzheimer's— and he wasn't the only one I would later learn. Of course, the bank wouldn't close the account for me without the power of attorney papers, the original ones, a multitude of forms and back and forth correspondences. Finally it closed, we paid off her credit card debt, sold her condo, and were free of Ian- financially.

And Kathy was wrong. Mum needed more than a babysitter.

Riversite in Wisconsin, 2001
The Other Side of the Door
by CNA (Certified Nursing Assistant) Cate

As a young mother, I worried when my young daughter was out of my sight. I feared an inattentive driver, someone talking on a car phone, might look away just as Christie wandered into the street, or that some recently released sexual predator might pass by the house just as my pretty three-year-old stood at the front door. Maybe he'd slow down and wave. Maybe she'd smile and wave back. Anything can happen in just those few seconds when *I wasn't there.*

So I had to be doubly sure my husband knew I was leaving the house before he got absorbed in his yard projects. "Christie's in the house sleeping. Be careful when you're mowing the lawn. She might get up and come outside. You know what a little adventurer she is."

Distracted by a lawn mower that didn't want to start, he answered but didn't look at me, "Don't worry; I wouldn't let anything happen to my princess."

"Be back in ten minutes. I'll expect you to have the house cleaned, too." That was just to see if he was listening at all.

"Okay," he said. So he wasn't listening.

I got into the car, picked up a sippy cup from the driver's seat and set it on the passenger side. Then I turned the key in the ignition, started first time. Pleased with the car's recently improved performance, I know I was smiling; I put the car in reverse, looked in the side view, but not the rearview, mirror and backed down the gravel driveway. Bumpy, I thought. Hope to have it blacktopped this summer. I would have looked in the rearview mirror then but...

"Nooooooo," Tom howled, the sound of agony.

I spun my head around toward the direction his voice.

"She's in the driveway!"

I froze for a split second. Just enough time to make a decision. I put the car back in drive and stepped on the accelerator. For that, my husband never forgave me. I had run over our daughter twice. Miraculously, she did survive. Our marriage did not.

I was the talk of the family for years. They supported me, of course, and so did my friends, at least on the surface, but they didn't ask me to baby sit or drive their kids anywhere. And I didn't blame them. I couldn't forgive myself.

Aunt Jessie saved me from losing myself when my parents were killed in a car accident when I was 14 years old. She finished raising me, told me, "I'm your mother now. Don't call me Aunt Jessie anymore. Call me Mom." So I did. "Mom" saved me from losing myself a second time after my horrible mistake in the driveway.

"You made a mistake, a big one, but you have to stay together for her. No one contested your having custody of Christie because everyone knows you are a fine mother and a fine person. Your daughter survived. Now, you have to survive, too."

Unlike some other people who knew my personal history, Mom thought I'd make a wonderful nurse, someone who took care of others; she had uncanny faith in me. "You're a natural. Now, lead with your head. Do what is in your nature to do. Besides, there's a nurse shortage now. You'll be able to work anywhere you want, always have a job." I couldn't afford the college work required to become a registered nurse; she offered to help me financially. But this widow with health problems and plenty of expenses shouldn't have to bail me out again. What little money she had she'd need; I couldn't accept the offer.

I enrolled in a Certified Nursing Assistant program, short and inexpensive and likely to lead me to a full time job with health coverage for me and Christie.

Things turned out well initially. I was a full time CNA hired by Riversite Healthcare Center. The complex had a child care center, an immeasurably helpful perk for me and Christie. Meanwhile, Mom, who was used to some chronic health issues including diabetes and heart disease, began to exhibit signs of Alzheimer's. She didn't forget her car keys; she forgot she had a car. She couldn't remember her address or her own phone number. She set off the smoke alarm in her kitchen when she'd leave scrambled eggs cooking on the stove. The fire department would show up and she couldn't explain what happened. And the worst, she got lost at a shopping mall and couldn't tell anyone where she lived. That involved the police. After her official diagnosis of Alzheimer's, her two kids, both out of state, pleaded with me to get her admitted to Riversite as a resident and I did. Although I wasn't assigned her care, Riversite policy, I could see her each day. She'd been a safety net for me more than once. Now it was my turn.

–2001–

I take her out of the building when I'm not working. As long as she can still get around— she's not in a wheelchair yet—I can enrich her life, include her in family gatherings, and keep her involved with my daughter. But geographic change confuses Alzheimer's victims, so returning to the Riversite building challenges me and Mom. Sometimes she doesn't remember she lives here. Or she is intimidated by some residents, like one man in a wheelchair who used to sit outside in front of the Riversite entrance. His very thin body but hugely protruding stomach suggested liver disease. He'd leer at Mom as we came and went. I didn't like the way his eyes scanned her body. He might have been a lecher, and he was probably admitted to dry out, substance abuse. He doesn't sit there leering anymore. I don't know what happened to him. I'd be surprised if he's still alive.

A woman, not even middle aged chronologically but worn and haggard in the face, lived on Mom's wing until recently. She resided in a room by herself mainly because one roommate demanded to be moved and the other one left the nursing home entirely, and the staff seemed reluctant to put anyone else in there. But one of Mom's CNAs thought moving her to Renie's room would solve a few problems. Mom's deaf roommate and her assorted healthcare devices—oxygen machine, commode, walker and wheelchair—crowded the room, created obstacles to Mom's movements. Renie was not wheelchair bound and the configuration of her room was without obstacles.

It was an interesting proposition, but the social worker said she didn't think Renie would be a good match for Mom. She didn't elaborate, and she knew something she wasn't sharing. Family is privy to medical information about their own loved one, but not to medical information about other residents. They are protected by privacy laws, and my role today was family of Jessie, not CNA. Renie's CNA thought the match would work. All I knew was the door to her room was always closed and it wasn't staff who were closing it. What did Renie have to hide?

My family had designated me as Mom's medical power of attorney, partly because I worked in the facility. They may have thought I owed it to her for taking me in after my parents died. Then again, maybe none of them wanted the job. I decided to investigate myself and meet the mystery resident. The CNA knocked on her door and opened it simultaneously.

"Renie, this is Jessie and Cate. Jessie is thinking of becoming your roommate."

Renie glared suspiciously at me, "Does she get up at night?"

Then she interrogated Mom, "You remember me, don't you, Jessie? I sat at your table," But there was no warmth in the inquiry, no smile. And when people say to Mom, "Don't you remember?" my mood gets ugly. I had a bad feeling and didn't pursue this. Mom likes to have her TV on, loud, and I guessed this woman might have a problem with that, too. Plus, Mom's been presented with the prospect of moving to another room before. She says, "Oh I get along fine with my roommate." She's afraid of change, of course.

Rumor was Renie was dying of cancer; that's what one CNA told me. But Renie was there for months and months and didn't seem dying to me. Sometimes she would stop me in the hall. "Your mother is really a sweet lady. I think she is smiling a little more lately, too." Or she'd say, "I think your mother is a little less confused lately, and I'm not just saying that. If you ever want to know how she is really doing,

ask me. If you ask the staff, they'll just tell you what you want to hear."
She didn't consider me "staff," but I did agree with her assessment, so
Renie became my secret sentinel.

I think she just didn't want a roommate. Medicaid patients can't
have a private room. Self-paying patients can but pay much more. I
think Renie was paying for a half room but getting a full, private room
by driving people away. She wasn't worried about having to share a
room with Mom anymore, and I wasn't a CNA on her wing or an
administrator, so Renie approved of me; a mutual trust developed. I
enjoyed having a resident contact on Mom's wing.

Sometimes the two of us would commiserate about staff that we
considered incompetent or too ornery for this kind of work. We had
pet names for staff and labels for staff speed: slow and slower in some
cases. Known to others as Tilly, Atilla, we giggled, was the worst and
slowest. Renie said she was awfully glad she didn't have to depend on
that woman when she needed to go to the bathroom. I noticed that
she neglected to pick up Mom's laundry, that she barked at people.
There are CNAs who smile at residents; those smiles can lower blood
pressure and enhance mood better than Zoloft or Prosac. Conversely,
residents already feeling incarcerated don't welcome a grumbling or
distracted caregiver in the space of their little half-rooms. Renie and I
used each other for reciprocal venting, and she predicted that in not
too long I'd lock horns with the one we called Atilla.

In fact, though, I try to work things out with fellow staff rather
than create problems for them. I know how hard the job is. CNAs at
Riversite aren't paid well ($12,000-20,000 a year) and our job is both
physically and emotionally demanding. We appreciate support just like
everybody else, and many residents, especially if they're uncomfortable
and sick, don't welcome our efforts. On the other hand, when staffing

is inadequate or weak staff are not closely supervised, caregivers can create a kind of triage, and I hate this ugly reality. They can't or won't finish all their assignments, so they are tempted to provide minimal care to those least likely to register a complaint. And the least likely to complain are those who have no memory or those who have no voice. In the case of Mom, her care needs have increased since she was first admitted. New aides—and there is a lot of turnover—need to be educated to her needs, even though the needs are spelled out in her care plan. For example, Mom is supposed to be given assistance with dressing in the morning; she doesn't change her underwear. If an aide lays out fresh underwear on her bed, Mom just puts it away. Or she gets dressed before the aide comes in, skipping the underpants change. Sometimes she puts a fresh pair on over an old pair. It must be communicated clearly to the aide that she has to physically remove the old underwear, check for incontinence, etc., and place the fresh underwear on her. Tilly was fully aware of that care plan, but Mom became the victim of CNA triage.

She stayed in her room one day instead of going to the dining room for lunch, said she didn't feel well. Not feeling well isn't unusual but not going to the dining room is. Before I start my shift in the morning, I mark Mom's underwear with a permanent marker so I know the next morning if it's been changed. If she is uncomfortable, she is anxious, then nauseous. I suspected the underwear. There was the mark on her brief. I asked CNA Tilly if she had changed Mum's underwear that morning. I knew the answer but wanted catch her in a lie. She said no, that the staff on her wing were shorthanded, had been for three days, and she had 13 residents—norm on her wing is 10—to attend to and that another aide had failed to show up for work. She was irritated and not at all sympathetic to Mom or apologetic. I took Mom's lunch tray to her room myself, set it down, picked up her telephone, called Riversite and asked for the director of nursing; she was my boss as well as Tilly's so this was awkward.

I described the incident and repeated Tilly's assessment of her predicament. The director seemed concerned and protested the we are short staffed part, didn't agree with that. Later, I learned that Tilly was written up, some kind of disciplinary thing and had been moved to a different wing. Not removed, just moved, luckily not to my wing. And I think I was regarded as a bit of a pariah around the place.

Shortly after, my secret sentinel disappeared. At Mom's staffing, I asked the social worker what happened to Renie. She said, "She left Riversite," but offered no explanation. Privacy law. I already knew, though, what went on behind Renie's closed door because there is no law that says residents can't talk. She was at Riversite to dry out. Her closed door hid her solo happy hours which were purportedly many and occurred anytime of the day or night. That's why the social worker believed she and Mom weren't a good match. Word on the wing— miraculously, Renie's condition improved anyway; she found an apartment and moved out. I told the social worker I was just curious about Renie because I had grown to like her.

The social worker said, "We wish her well." I think they were glad to be rid of her.

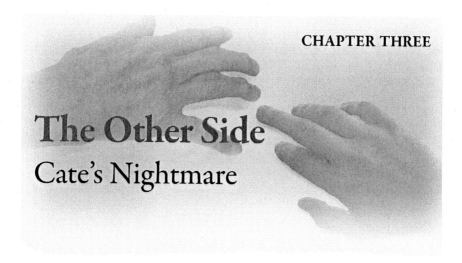

CHAPTER THREE

The Other Side
Cate's Nightmare

—Riversite, 2001—

The setting: *Jessie's niece/daughter, on her day off from CNA duties, enters Riversite through its elegant lobby. Beyond that area, which has been designed to please visitors, is the door to the residential area, the dining room first. Residents are seated around circular tables set for four. Some residents are in stationary chairs, most are in wheelchairs, a few in Broda chairs. We focus now on the table in front of the window. Seated there, Dee (resident Alzheimer's victim, married to John) has moved her food from her plate to the tabletop as her husband, who visits daily, looks on. Across from John is Bonnie (blind and nervous woman whose husband used to take care of her, but he has been hospitalized). Bonnie has been placed here until her family figures out what to do. To her right is Jessie (resident Alzheimer's victim, widow).*

John has just noticed that at a table to the far east of his, a female resident has tumbled forward and died. The staff in the room gallop past diners to whisk the deceased from the scene. As they brush past the window table of four:

23

Bonnie, *with emphasis on the who*: "Who's there? Who's there?"

Jessie, *emphasis on where*: "Who's where? Who's where?"

John, *not wanting to alarm his wife or others*: "They're just taking a sick resident back to her room."

Bonnie, *increasingly agitated*: "Where'd they go? Where'd they go?"

Dee is smiling at her peas.

Jessie, *befuddled*: "*What?*"

Bonnie: "Who was it? Who was it?"

Jessie, *her face contorted in confusion*: "What? Who are you talking about?"

John, wishing to change the subject: "Dee, are you going to take all day to eat your lunch?"

Dee, *offended, scowls as she grabs her applesauce*: "Drop dead!"

Jessie is perplexed but would be no matter what the conversation and doesn't care anyway as she has finished her meal and is ready to leave. John reminds her to take her walker and Jessie begins her shuffle through the dining room. Her advocate, Cate, greets her in the hallway but is not happy to see that one of the skis on Jessie's walker has broken off, perhaps run over by a marauding wheelchair or crushed by the big paw of the certified nursing assistant (CNA) whom residents have aptly named Atilla da honey(for her combative personality) or bitten off by the CNA nicknamed Rotty Weiller (for her snarl).

Leaving Riversite with Cate, Jessie waits for the automatic door to open and moves forward. She is unsteady and unaware that she doesn't lift her feet when she walks; this is her Alzheimer's shuffle. She does not look down, her focus is straight ahead. Her broken ski hooks on the door mat and she tumbles forward. Cate catches her before she hits the ground.

Jessie: "That scared me."

Cate, in an aside, rolls her eyes and vents: "She's had at least six falls that I know of. One fall landed her in the hospital, staples in her head. Now her head contains no memory of any of that, she has a walker that is a safety hazard, and I can't get anyone's attention."

Cate, *recovering her patience*: "Let's go to the physical therapy room."

Therapist #1: "Oh, let's see. There isn't a ski here that fits this walker."

Cate: "I see some walkers have tennis balls instead of skis. Could we try those?"

Therapist #1: "I don't know where there are any tennis balls. I'll just write myself a note to have somebody fix this walker on Tuesday."

Cate: "Not fix it until Tuesday? Today is Saturday."

Therapist #1: "It's the 4th of July weekend. No one will be here to do it until then."

So Cate leaves Riversite with Jessie, buys a tennis ball from Kmart, punctures the ball with a pocket knife, and shoves the leg of the walker into the ball, but it makes the walker pull to the left. Returning to

Riversite, Cate finds Myra the managing nurse and explains the episode.

Myra: "I can't believe they just sent you off like that without giving her a different walker. I've got a key; let's see what I can find. *They enter the cache of rehab equipment.* None of these is exactly the right height, but we can adjust one. I'll leave a note to have them fix Jessie's walker on Tuesday."

They successfully conduct their raid and Jessie has a suitable but temporary replacement.

Tuesday

Cate approaches room 118 hoping the repaired walker will be in Jessie's room. Alas, it is not. She and Jessie head once again to P.T.

Therapist # 2: "We don't have a ski for it."

Cate: "Her walker is hanging on the wall. That's all you did with it, just hang it up?"

Therapist # 2: "Well, I could take the other ski off and put a tennis ball on the bottom of each leg."

This is what the therapist does.

Thursday

Cate: "Are you still having trouble steering your walker?"

Jessie: "It wants to go the other way."

Cate inspects the walker. The left wheel has been attached to the outside leg and the right wheel has been attached to the inside.

Cate: "Back to therapy we go."

Therapist # 3 corrects the wheels, but the tennis balls cause the walker to drag.

Cate: "Back to therapy."

This time therapist #4 puts plugs into the bottom of the walker where the skis and then the tennis balls used to be. One plug is securely in, the other isn't. Cate bangs the walker into the floor to secure both plugs.

Cate wonders why P.T doesn't just issue Jessie a new walker. Miraculously, at that moment, the very popular CNA Joy appears.

Cate: "Can't P.T. issue a better walker than this? Where are walkers with four wheels?"

Joy, *smiling*: "You know, WalMart has a four-wheel walker on sale. It even has a seat so Jessie can sit down if she is tired. Maybe you could get one of those."

And that is what Cate does.

ఆ‑ఆ‑ఆ‑ఆ‑ఆ‑ఆ‑ఆ‑ఆ‑ఆ‑ఆ‑ఆ‑ఆ‑ఆ‑ఆ‑ఆ‑ఆ‑ఆ‑ఆ‑ఆ

Now Jessie, with her shiny new walker, happily flies down the halls of Riversite as she can't remember the new walker has hand brakes. Occasionally a physical therapist greets her with, "Slow down, Jessie," or "How are you, Jessie?"

Jessie: "I'm staying alive."

A visitor pushing a stroller passes Jessie. Jessie, startled and mesmerized by the lovely baby tucked inside, lets go of her walker and turns to coo at the little darling. Residents and staff alike see Jessie without her walker; they rush as fast as nursing home residents and staff can. One man takes one arm, a woman takes the other, and a third rescuer grabs Jessie's walker. The three of them unite Jessie with her shiny flier and save her from a fall.

Jessie, dancing on and singing her theme song: "Stayin' alive, stayin' alive. Ah, ha, ha, ha, stayin' aliiiivvvve...."

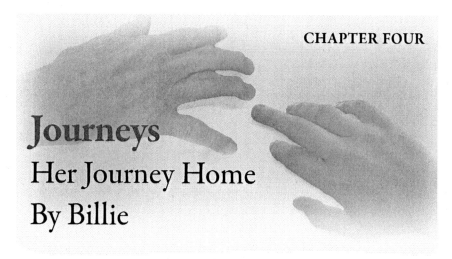

CHAPTER FOUR

Journeys
Her Journey Home
By Billie

–Wisconsin, 2001-2002–

I feel human again," Mum said while disembarking from her Florida-Wisconsin flight, an airport attendant easing her into a wheelchair. She was, in fact, on her way to feeling well again, but this airport was just the first stop of a convoluted journey to dementia and institutional care. None of us could anticipate the bumps along the way or her ultimate destination.

Once in Wisconsin and moved into my house, the search for some answers began. We consulted an internist, a blood specialist and a neurologist. Mum's red blood cell count had plummeted, so much that doctors didn't understand how she could be conscious much less walking. Blood loss from internal bleeding caused the drop. She had three colonoscopies before it was determined that severe diverticulosis was the culprit and that blood had poured into the colon. For now it had stopped, and the goal was to build her back up after having lost 40 pounds and a lot of blood, and all this was before seeing the neurologist about her memory.

On Oct. 12, 2001, Mum met her neurologist who diagnosed the source of her dementia. Alzheimer's cannot be categorically identified without a brain biopsy and that can't occur until after death, so the science of diagnosing Alzheimer's is not as exact as we would like. The report included this:

...A CT scan of the brain without contrast showed some modest atrophy without any definite focal areas of infarct but some mild, diffuse, decreased attenuation in the paraventricular regions.

Infarct means vascular disease, hemorrhaging in the brain, and attenuation means weakening or thinning. Simply put, evidence of a brain hemorrhage could not be observed and that was ruled out.

The patient underwent a Cognistate evaluation. ... showed a significant impairment in memory and orientation, with relative preservation in other areas of cognition.

The Cognistate evaluation assesses intellectual function in language, construction ability, memory, calculation skills, reasoning and judgment.

This patient scored normal or nearly normal in all areas except memory and orientation... This pattern of memory impairment is quite specific for memory and is not as broad as might be expected in a typical Alzheimer's patient. ... The impairment of memory does appear to be quite severe, however.

Mum's memory function was severely abnormal but other cognition was better than expected for an Alzheimer's victim. Mum told me the doctor asked a lot of questions. "I think I did pretty well, though. The doctor was impressed." What may have impressed the doctor and misled Mum is that her ability to think in the moment was good. The real news, in fact, was bad. Memory loss that is caused by drugs or depression can be restored. If the loss is caused by stroke, the damage might be limited, but if it's a dementing disease like Alzheimer's, the victims don't recover. They always decline. Already Mum's short term memory loss and orientation were profound.

Because she hadn't as yet recognized her own incompetence and because Ian didn't accept the Alzheimer's diagnosis—denial is very common in these cases—moving back to Florida was definitely in her plans. Both he and Mum tried to enlist the support of other relatives to have my sister and I persuaded likewise. Some of the relatives doubted the diagnosis. From one uncle, "She sounds fine to me."

ぐぐぐぐぐぐぐぐぐぐぐぐぐぐぐぐぐぐぐ

Perusing old photo albums is a pleasant pastime for Mum and me. One afternoon, the phone rang in her bedroom. Not aware of the ringing, she reamined focused on the photos. I reminded her to answer the phone. She looked happy with whomever it was, so I assumed it was Ian.

She said, "Well, I'm here at, well, 'Billie, where am I? What is this place?'"

"It's my house."

She said, "It's Billie's house; I'm at Billie's." And, "Billie is here with me. My daughter Billie is here. Oh, she doesn't' mind." Then, "Okay, love you too, bye."

I asked, "Was that Ian?"

"I don't know. I can't remember."

That's the severity of short term memory loss.

ఆ-ఆ-ఆ-ఆ-ఆ-ఆ-ఆ-ఆ-ఆ-ఆ-ఆ-ఆ-ఆ-ఆ-ఆ-ఆ-ఆ-ఆ

Orientation shortcomings mean she cannot identify things like the current day, month, year, season, her own phone number or address, who is president, who we're at war with, whether or not she ate lunch, where she lives, whether or not she is married, etc. She also can't orient herself to relationships to people.

This is one example of Mum's confusion about who I am. While on an afternoon drive, she asked, "We aren't related are we?"

"Well, yes we are. I am your daughter and you are my mother."

"What? Really?"

"Yes, you had three kids: Jimmy then Billie then Anne. I'm Billie."

"Oh, then Jimmy is your brother."

"Yes."

"He must be a big kid by now."

"He had leukemia. He died when he was 12." She couldn't remember.

Once back at my home, "Where do I live? Do I live here? Do I have clothes here? Will you come in with me?" she repeats. She is afraid because she does not recognize the place she has been living for a year.

"Does my mother come to see me here?"

꧁꧂꧁꧂꧁꧂꧁꧂꧁꧂꧁꧂꧁꧂꧁꧂꧁꧂꧁꧂꧁꧂

Among other things, the neurologist report noted this understatement: She is extremely forgetful, and she has to be reminded to take a shower. The fact is she stopped taking showers altogether, and that started in Florida, not unusual for the elderly and especially for Alzheimer's patients; they don't like to get wet. For example, Mum typically protests showers, won't take them herself although she says she does. She needs help because she can't operate the faucets, differentiate between hot and cold, keep her balance, remember which part of her has been washed or whether she has rinsed her hair, etc.

So on one typical occasion with a little persistence, I got her into the shower stall. Once lathered up, she protested soap and water getting into her eyes.

I rinsed her face and then she squealed, "Oh, Billie!" like I was torturing her. "I'm drowning!"

"Mum, is the water too hot or too cold?"

"Both!"

Afterwards, while combing out her hair, "How does that feel?"

"That feels good!"

And she had no recall about recoiling over the mere suggestion of a shower.

The severity of memory loss manifests itself at Christmas. When Mum opens a present, she says, "Oh, this is lovely," then puts it down for about 20 seconds. Then she picks it up again and asks who it is for. She has already forgotten. This year I wrapped presents for her for each of three family get-togethers on three consecutive days. After each day, I rewrapped her presents to open again the next day. Each time was a first for her.

❧❧❧❧❧❧❧❧❧❧❧❧❧❧❧❧❧❧❧❧

The neurologist's summary: *Based on the relatively gradual, progressive nature of the complaints, the lack of other neurologic signs and the severity of memory impairment, a primary dementing illness such as Alzheimer's is a strong consideration. This patient's dementia is likely Alzheimer's..., and I have recommended that she start on Excelon 1.5 mg bid and then, in a month, go to three mg bid.*

So, back in 2001, Mum started to eat again and regain weight. Her red blood cell count improved. My husband and I locked up our medications after noticing bottles of aspirin disappearing from our bedroom and winding up in Mum's room. She had no idea how they got there. We had no idea how many she took.

She did regain weight, but there was no recovery of memory and her anxiety continued to bubble up. Sometimes, when I was at work, she'd call and leave 25 or more messages on my voice mail, calls made in a 20 minute period. My retired husband might have been mowing the lawn or taking a shower; he was nearby. But, if Mum had no one in close physical proximity, she was alone as far as she was concerned. These were her panic attacks.

Mum's anxiety had not been addressed by the neurologist. Her pre-Alzheimer's medical history included bouts with an anxiety neurosis. So Ativan and Zoloft-for anxiety and depression- were added and adjusted periodically. After noting an increase in confusion, a psychiatrist added another medication to the mix—Namenda (known as memantine, it is first of a new class of drugs). Namenda can be used for patients with moderate to severe Alzheimer's. Benefits: It can provide some psychomotor functioning benefit. It can slow the decline of daily living skills, like the ability to hold a fork.

But side effects include dizziness, agitation, confusion, headache and constipation. Already confused, agitated, suffering from bouts of nausea related to anxiety, dizziness causing balance problems, Mum was prescribed a medication that had been demonstrated to cause more confusion, agitation and dizziness in some patients. So the internist, in concordance with our family's wishes and against the wishes of the psychiatrist, took Mum off both Excelon and Namenda. Within 48 hours she was noticeably less agitated.

❧❧❧❧❧❧❧❧❧❧❧❧❧❧❧❧❧❧❧❧❧

"Is someone going to take me home?"

"What do you mean by home?"

"You know... home."

"Do you mean Lake Foxbrook?"

"Yes."

I could see Mum's agitation developing, her scanning the room but not recognizing it, eyes widening, inability to comprehend. She drifts in and out of these moments, can't reason through them. These anxious feelings can be ameliorated with a story she can connect with, so I told her a Lake Foxbrook story, hoping to deflect her fear. She still had memories of her life 45 years ago but not 45 minutes ago.

"Mum, when I was in the 5th grade in Lake Foxbrook , I thought we were 'poor people,' but not in the sense of no food or shelter or broken family or trailer park living. It was my wardrobe. I wore the same clothes over and over which would have been fine if that's what everyone at school was doing. But I went to public schools—no uniforms like you had when you were in school. That meant everyone knew—look at the clothes—who had money and who didn't.

"Two girls from my middle school days stood out as spectacular students, good looking and adorned in lovely clothes, never wearing the same thing two days in a row. I looked like a sixth grader when I was one, a chubby one, too. They looked like teenage models. Both of them were unique; one very German and one very Greek. I was just a dork. I too was the child of an immigrant, you being Scottish, Mum. But not affluent. They were.

"I asked you once if I had any royal blood, your ancestry in the British Isles and all. You told me you thought not, that probably my ancestors were sheep thieves. I imagined Thaya- the-Greek's ancestors to be raven-haired goddesses of Mt. Olympus, the kind I learned about in literature. Dad's side of our family hail back to Nancy Hanks, Abraham Lincoln's mother. That's sort of royal, in an American way, but that Kentucky branch of the family also happened to make its living manufacturing moonshine. Plus, Mum, Dad's grandfather got into a tavern brawl with his brother-in-law. This is part of family lore. They fought over oxen yoke. Great Grandpa killed the guy, went to prison, was born again and then a minister somehow orchestrated his release. So I'm related to a born again drunken murderer. I imagined Maude-the-German's father being some gentrified owner of baronial estates.

38

So we had nothing in common, I thought.

"That year, Jimmy [my brother] died; you bought me a new dress for the funeral which I later wore at school. A very kind teacher, Mrs. Schwagel, commented on how lovely my dress was. Andy Warhol might call this my 15 minutes of fame. It lasted about 15 seconds. Rather than bask in admiring glances, I endured Maudie's distain, her evil eyes scanning my dress. Thaya allowed me a view of her facial profile, nose stuck high in the air. She's not supposed to be receiving attention I imagined she thought. We were not on the same playing field in the socioeconomic or good looks department. But this was a public school and the true equalizer was—as it should be—academic performance. We were on the same playing field in the cerebral department.

"I didn't like speaking up in class. I had no confidence, painfully aware of my nondescript presence and my chubbiness—fat has never been de rigueur. It wasn't that I was an atrocity; it was more that I was invisible, like a senior citizen on a Florida beach during spring break. A piece of driftwood commands more respect. But even in the 5th grade, I knew the difference between succeed and secede. As part of a history lesson, Mr. Bruin asked, 'What was the real cause of the Civil War?'

"Thaya answered, of course. 'The South wanted to succeed from the Union,' she demurred.

"She was wrong! Thaya made a mistake and I was witness! Didn't the teacher catch it? Won't someone say something? Dare I say anything? I did. I raised my thank-God-for-public-education- in-America-poor-person-trembling, chubby hand and declared, 'The South wanted to secede from the Union.'

"And the grinning teacher could not conceal his surprise, actually delight. My inferiority, my second class status, lower caste complexes momentarily vanished. But that wasn't enough to satisfy me. I blurted, 'So Thaya is wrong.' Thaya glared; she actually granted me eye contact! I could have burst my big fat seams with joy. Halleluiah and bring it on. I had arrived."

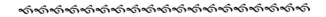

"Oh, Billie, you are a character."

"I know, but I bet you're feeling pretty good."

"What?"

"Mum, you are testament to the medicinal power of story. And you know after the Thaya and Maudie days, you took me to see Dr. Laskow and he helped me lose weight. Thanks for that, Mum."

"You mean you used to be fat?"

CHAPTER FIVE

Journeys
Last Days of Blanche Dubois
Journaled by Cate

JULY 20, 2001

I've known Jessie, my aunt and second mother, forever and Blanche for four years, the four years she's been Jessie's roommate at Riversite. I'd describe their relationship as one of mutual tolerance. Mom's been diagnosed with Alzheimer's but her personality hasn't changed, at least not yet. She likes privacy. Blanche likes privacy too, so keeping the room's dividing drapes drawn doesn't offend either. Mom has to cross through Blanche's space to get to the bathroom and hallway, though. Sometimes Blanche is in the middle of the passageway. Mom says quietly, "Excuse me, Blanche," but Blanche is almost deaf, so unless she sees Mom coming, she doesn't move her chair, or she moves it ever so slowly. Mom does not remember Blanche's deafness, so she believes Blanche is intentionally aloof and uncooperative. She tries to squeeze by and Blanche, alarmed, yelps something unfriendly. Mom glares. And that's how it goes.

Mom and Blanche's room is on the first floor of what had been a long term care unit. But the needs of those patients have changed. Some residents who were admitted for physical problems have developed cognitive problems, too, so first floor also houses a cluster of residents with dementia afflictions. Mom was convinced when we first moved her into room 118 that the room had a vacancy because Blanche had driven out previous roommates. She said the aides turned on lights in the middle of the night to tend to Blanche's needs. They were noisy and didn't respect Mom's need for sleep, she believed. But staff insisted that some lights needed to be turned on so aides could see what they were doing, and I concurred, but I wondered whether they were quiet during the cares as we caregivers call our work. Blanche is deaf but Mom isn't. I brought ear plugs and an eye patch for Mom and hunted for another room. Each time she was shown a room, Mom balked. She did not want to move. Later, Blanche moved to a different room. She was back to 118 in two days. She said her new roommate hit her and was just "evil." Blanche said she was glad to be "home."

Now 95, Blanche is always in her wheelchair. There is a walker in her room but she doesn't use it, is physically unable to. She used to use it but even when she could stand, her body bent in half. Blanche's infirmity, in addition to her advanced age, is severe osteoporosis. Her bones are so frail, she suffered broken ribs from a mammogram her niece Sophia, the only person who visits Blanche, once told me.

To eliminate obstacles, staff collapsed Blanche's walker and stored it in a closet. Blanche went BALLISTIC over that. She wants her walker and she wants it in the space it has always occupied. No flexibility in body or in mind. Speaking of mind. Blanche may be nearly deaf and have no teeth, not even dentures anymore because her gums are too soft, but her mind and memory, unlike Mom's, are usually sharp. Except for today. When I walked into the room, an unusually agitated Blanche pointed to a calendar on the north wall and screeched, "Look at that!"

I said, "Your calendar?"

Increasingly frustrated, she barked, "No, no. The wall, the scribbling all over the wall. There, there!" Blanche used her demanding tone with staff. I had on my CNA uniform so she had at me.

I looked directly at an off white, unadorned wall, no writing that I could see. So I put my finger on the wall and inquired, "Do you mean here?"

"Yes, all over there."

"Blanche, there is no writing here that I can see."

"Do you wear glasses?" she shrieked. "You need them!"

Blanche having a bad day.

DECEMBER 25, 2001

Blanche has an electric bed now. Merry Christmas. The old fashioned version has three crank handles at the base of one end of the bed. Those cranks are turned to move the mattress various ways, and they are designed to be tucked under the bed when not in use. I reminded Mom's aides who repeatedly left the cranks out, to tuck them under. They are a potential tripping hazard for residents and staff. Mom used to have bruises on her shins that I couldn't figure out until I saw those cranks out; in my part of the building, the beds are all electric. Mom must have banged right into those handles. And even the social worker gave up on aides being up to the task and just ordered an electric bed for Blanche- no cranks, all push button. Eventually, all beds are going to be electric, I am told; who gets them first is probably political.

MARCH 9, 2002

This is kind of a first. Mom and I navigated around Blanche and out of the room. When we returned a few hours later, she was sitting in her wheelchair off to one side instead of in the middle of the passageway. She looked up amicably as we entered, "I knew you were coming." That was nice.

MARCH 20, 2002

Blanche is down to 88 pounds, really skeletal. She complains about how this and that hurts when the aides put her to bed. What hurts Blanche wouldn't hurt most of us. Her osteo has resulted in frail bones and the weight loss includes loss of muscle, so she can do nothing to assist in her own movement. The staff have to use the assistance of a crane to safely lift her. Now she has an upper urinary track infection and appears to eat just a few teaspoonfuls of food a day. Blanche's been down with ailments before, but it seems lately she might be at the end. An aide who has known Blanche for a long time thinks Blanche is just plain tired of living. Certainly she must be tired of how everything hurts.

The last two summers, I brought her zinnias from my garden. Flowers, that's how to exact a smile from Blanche. She could sit for a long time and just take in those flowers, sweet little grin on her face. She told me once, "I'm lucky I know you." I kept producing flowers for both Mom and Blanche as long as my garden cooperated. That won't start again for a few more months. I wonder if Blanche will still be here. I do see flowers on Blanche's table now, though, from her niece.

MARCH 21, 2002

Blanche is still in bed but alert enough to wave back when I wave to her.

MARCH 25, 2002

I called Mom about 6:30 p.m.; she was just getting into bed, said she was going to try to sleep. I heard a woman's voice. It was Blanche's niece trying to talk to Blanche in the volume (very loud) that Blanche can hear. I imagine this isn't exactly a lullaby for Mom. I stayed on the phone with her a while, but she seemed distracted; then said she needed to go to the bathroom.

MARCH 27, 2002

Met Mom after her lunch. Blanche's niece was in the room. She's visiting more often lately. She used to visit weekly, I think (still a lot more attention than some residents get). She said Blanche didn't like the hearing devices she got for her, didn't like things in her ears.

I heard Blanche complain to her niece that nobody talks to her. None of the four people at her table converses. They may be hard of hearing, may be depressed, uncomfortable. It's hard to know with some residents. Blanche does chatter away to her niece, though.

MARCH 28, 2002

Blanche's niece told me that Blanche was a little better today, eating liquid food, but that on the weekend, the hospice nurse thought Blanche would not last the week. I'm sure Sophia, the niece, has mixed feelings about Blanche's survival at age 96 in the shape she's in, knowing she's miserable and alone most of the time. All I could say was, "This must be so hard for you. Good luck."

She asked Mom how she was. "I'm staying alive." That's Mom's generic answer to questions about her well being. I guess she's got a point.

Mom seems a little insecure lately when I leave. I do believe Blanche's situation has unnerved her a bit.

MARCH 30, 2002

Passage into Mom's room is blocked by a new and huge Broda chair for Blanche who was up for the first time in a week. Broda chairs are for patients who have balance or mobility disabilities. The seat can pivot, tilt and suspend the user's weight across multiple points. Blanche graduated to the giant chair because she was sliding out of her previous wheelchair. She is so weak, she can't keep herself upright, even in a chair. When the hallway flooring at Riversite was being replaced, Blanche leaned forward and bent over to pick up bits of debris from the old tiles. One day, when I was in the room, four different staff stopped to remind Blanche not to do that; she might fall out of her chair. They assured her that the workmen would pick up all the debris. Then Blanche would go right back to tidying up. She protested when the idea of being strapped in her chair was introduced. Said she didn't need that. She did, though. So now she is in the giant chair, more like a bed on wheels, half lying down, half sitting.

Mom can walk past the big chair but not with her walker, and she needs that walker when she leaves the room! A CNA said she would move Blanche's bed against the wall to create more space. I don't know why that hasn't been done already. Myra, an administrator, told the CNA to push Blanche's chair further back, still hasn't been done. My frustration level is commensurate with my blood pressure, both elevated.

I have such a bad feeling leaving Mom there when I have no confidence that her needs are being met, especially now that Blanche's needs are so great. Unfortunately, when you are a caregiver assigned 10-13 residents, the residents aren't going to get much care, unless the resident gets very sick. That resident, Blanche in this case, will get more care than the others, and the others include Mom, unfortunately. So I have been ducking down here during my lunch and on breaks to check on Mom.

MARCH 31, 2002

Mom called last night which is unusual. She didn't know why she called, but there was anxiety. "This place. Why am I here? I'm in the hospital but I'm not sick." I went through her medical history and her need for assistance and her memory problems. She concurred that her memory is bad, wicked she called it, and wanted to know when she takes her medication. I told her the nurses give it to her even though she doesn't remember. And then the big question and what's really behind her anxiety, "Well, I'm not dying or anything, am I?"

"No, Mom, you're just stuck with a bad memory. But call me any time you have questions about something you can't remember."

"Okay, I'll have to remember that."

Mom has sometimes wondered why she is "in the hospital" if she isn't sick. She knows she's mortal, like the rest of us, but like the rest of us, she doesn't think much about dying until death appears imminent. I imagine a roommate as near to death as Blanche might bring her to the conclusion that she too is on death row.

And I'm not sure what Mom has heard in conversations about Blanche's grave situation. Blanche may be nearly deaf, but Mom isn't. I'm not sure how careful the caregivers are about confidentiality or how sensitive they are to Mom right now. Hospice caregivers have visited. Blanche's niece says she hasn't talked to Blanche about her condition being terminal. That upper urinary tract infection plus her age, then congestive heart failure all converged to hasten her decline. Four years ago she had surgery after gangrene set in her toes. The surgeon warned that her age and frail condition made the surgery risky. The niece explained that to Blanche, and Blanche, taken by surprise, said, "You mean I might die?" Her niece reassured her that it was just a possibility and Blanche cried.

She survived that surgery, another one last year, and here she is still. Now Blanche says to her niece, "I just don't know." Does she just not know what's wrong with her or does she just not know if she wants to be alive anymore?

かかかかかかかかかかかかかかかかかかかかかか

At Riversite later, Mom in good spirits, engrossed in a movie. Blanche up and in her big chair, and her bed moved against the wall. Halleluiah. The niece was there and she seems to be visiting every day now. No wonder Blanche is rebounding.

かかかかかかかかかかかかかかかかかかかかかか

She reminds me a little of a former neighbor, an elderly and shriveled old man with a collection of cats and old appliances in his back yard. I watched from my front porch as John, hunched over and unkempt, pulled an empty red wagon with his gnarled hands, up the hill, then an hour or so later, down the hill, wagon laden with springs, car parts, cans, junk from I don't know where. He couldn't hear a thing, like Blanche. He always had a wave and a smile, though, like Blanche on a good day.

Once he needed a fuse for his basement, so he crossed over to my property and pounded hard on the door, too deaf to hear his own clamor. If I had been deaf, I'd have still known it was John. I'd feel the house rattle. Later the same day he returned, pummeled the door, and asked, "How old do you think I am?"

"Oh, about 70?" I flattered.

He was proud of himself. "I'm 93, and I'm pretty spry for my age."

That's all he wanted. Just to tell me his age. Of course, he was looking for company.

But the goodness of his intentions I learned not to doubt. I used to mow over an old stump embedded in my front lawn. One unfortunate day an angry band of hornets streamed out and enveloped me as I fled, leaving the running lawn mower unattended. I shed clothes as I ran through my house and into the shower where I washed the last nasty hornet down the drain. I was generously bitten. When I emerged from the house to face the venomous scene, there stooped over the lawn mower was John. He couldn't hear the engine and waved me over.

"Is the engine still running?"

I mouthed, "Yes, and there are hornets."

He stepped forward, pulled the mower from the nest and turned it off. The hornets, maybe exhausted now or not interested in John, largely dispersed.

John apologized profusely. He said he knew the hornets' nest was there, meant to tell me but forgot, having trouble remembering things lately. He had been watching me mow when he saw my panicked retreat into the house.

A few months later, when my house was for sale and I was preparing to relocate, John sent me a handwritten letter, hard to read, the geriatric scribble. He lamented that his son wanted to move him into a nursing home. John didn't want to leave, didn't want to give up his cats. He asked me to give him one room in my house, with a view of his yard so he could see his cats, and just two sausages a day. That's all he would need and he would put me in his will. I love old people like John; that's why I'm comfortable doing the work I do now, but there is no such thing as an elderly person who needs only two sausages a day and a room with a view. I wrote to John and explained that I had to move.

John did wind up in Good Hope Convalescence Center. That is where he died.

So here is Blanche in the same boat.

APRIL 2, 2002

I walked into room 118 while Mom was still in the dining room. Her privacy curtain had been pulled open and someone had moved Blanche so she was facing Mom's TV. Basically, Blanche was occupying the whole room. She can't move on her own, so an employee did this, maybe to watch TV as she fed Blanche.

There was a nurse in there—a hospice nurse—trying to talk to Blanche. I explained to the nurse that she had Blanche positioned to watch Mom's TV and that when she came back from lunch, she might like some privacy. The nurse looked around like she was seeing for the first time that the room is double occupancy. She did move Blanche back and closed the curtain, but what worries me is what would have been done or not done if I hadn't been there. So of course, I'll be spending my break time down here again tomorrow, shed my CNA identity for my advocate role.

When I returned to the room with Mom after her lunch, the aide was preparing to put Blanche back in bed—that's what Blanche wanted. But she was yelling, "Oh my God. Oooowwww. I just want to drop dead!" etc. I thought this would upset Mom. One other time, during the night shift, Blanche had cried out because, she claimed, an aide had pushed her into her bed and knocked over her water making her bed wet. She called out for help. Apparently, Mom summoned help. Later Blanche's niece complained, but the issue was settled at a meeting with an administrator and an ombudsperson who called it a he said she said case. The aide was assigned to a different wing and Mom was dismissed as "senile."

I suggested to Mom that we take a stroll while aides settled Blanche into bed. Mom protested and said she'd rather listen to Blanche than walk around. She doesn't like to walk now, takes so much focus. So we returned to her room, and I did the usual things like help her brush her dentures, comb her hair and look at old photos with her.

After Blanche was in bed, every few minutes she called for help. I fetched the daytime aide who is usually successful in getting Blanche to respond. She said she couldn't do anything more for her; Blanche wanted to go to bed, but she didn't want to eat, etc. Meanwhile, I tried to distract Mom with the photo album again. Sometimes her face reflects absolute bliss when she looks at old photos.

"Oh, look at that. That's my niece Cate. She was just like a daughter to me."

"That's me, when I was little."

"No, the other Cate. My niece Cate."

"Oh, that one."

But she would turn her head to hear Blanche's pleas and I asked her if that bothered her. She said, "No, I know she can't help it." I said I didn't think Blanche really needed help.

"I think she's a little out of her head." Mom agreed. But still, knowing she is listening to unanswered cries makes me feel sorrowful for Mom and for Blanche.

I went to Blanche's bedside a few times to speak to her. She said she didn't feel well. I couldn't find her nurse call button; it should have been easily accessible to Blanche. She quieted down when I was with her but when I returned to Mom's side of the room, she started up again, "Oh, my Gaawwd. Help me. Somebody help me." I've said it before. These people are lonely and just the distraction of another person with them relieves pain. If someone were just sitting with Blanche, she would rest quietly, I believe.

I'm dreading going back tomorrow. I'm afraid Blanche may be dead, and I'm afraid she may still be alive.

APRIL 3, 2002

Blanche still alive, but failing. It is amazing how long it can take to die. People will say Blanche died peacefully in her sleep. I think she may just be too weak to do anything else. Absence of movement doesn't necessarily mean absence of pain. I remember my pain when I had a colonoscopy. I was given some kind of intravenous drug cocktail to relax me; it was also a paralytic so I couldn't move, but I felt mega pain three times as the proctologist tried to push that little camera around the first main turn of my colon (blocked by adhesions caused by previous surgery I was to learn). I tried to scream; it may have come out a moan, or a grimace or maybe my blood pressure jumped up, and I'm sure the two doctors got some signal because my chart said they stopped the procedure because of extreme pain. My uncle in intensive care the week before he died looked peaceful, but he had beads of sweat forming on his forehead one day, and I don't know what he may have been feeling or dreaming. My conclusion is dying peacefully in bed is highly over rated.

Blanche was sleeping the whole afternoon, but whimpering a little. The social worker came into the room and said she didn't think there was much time left for Blanche. I was just glad Blanche wasn't calling out today. Mom seemed much better now, plus it was a sunny day, good for a country drive. Then I gave her a shower which she didn't like but quickly forgot. She didn't want me to leave. I lied and told her I'd be back in the evening; the lie won't be remembered and it helped her get through the moment.

APRIL 5, 2002

When I arrived at Mom's room, Blanche was in the big chair and all the drapes had been opened including Mom's privacy drape.

Blanche was with her niece when I left. Blanche seemed alert, waved to me when I waved to her. After yesterday, I can hardly believe she's alive much less sitting up.

APRIL 7, 2002

Blanche was up, getting attention from her niece, being fed lunch by her favorite aide, hospice person came in, etc. Privacy drapes had been opened; that is getting old from my point of view. I pulled them for Mom who was lying on her side on her bed with her back toward all the commotion. She was in good spirits, though, and we went out.

One of the residents who is wheelchair bound but fairly young and always friendly and cheerful told me on the way out that Mom had gone to lunch without her walker and at least three people jumped up and ran to her aid, one taking one arm, a second taking another arm while a third retrieved her walker. She said it was really sweet. Well, that's one for Riversite. I was glad to know that, especially this week with Mom getting kind of lost in the Blanche shuffle.

APRIL 12, 2002

Mom rounded a corner today and I mean that in a bad way. She was absolutely delusional. Here are some things that happened:

• She had trouble talking; first she couldn't talk at all. Then she spoke some sentences in gibberish.

• She tried to drink out of a Kleenex box that was full of Kleenex.

• She dropped her glasses, bent down to pick them up, and picked up a pair of shoes instead.

• She had trouble figuring out how to get her dentures out (for brushing).

• She went to lunch, turned around and went back to her room. I brought her a tray, had to practically feed her. She couldn't hold a spoon. She made quite a mess, partly because I didn't have a bib for her.

• I helped her change tops three times because she spilled coffee on herself so many times. She choked and spit up a lot.

• She went to dinner but then left to go back to her room, only she didn't get to her room. She wandered into a man's room and when the man came back from dinner, he found her in his bed!

• I drove back to Riversite that night to check on her. She had dollar bills on her person, three of them. I don't know where they came from, maybe that guy's room.

I got Mom to urinate in a little tray so her urine could be tested for infection- no infection. Urinary tract infections can cause delusions. The nurse called tonight and said the doctor ordered more lab tests tomorrow. The nurse said it may be the progression of the dementia. Sometimes people do a big plunge very quickly, she said. That didn't resonate with me. We'll see tomorrow. I'm kind of scared. The deterioration was significant. I am sure Mom did not know who I was although that's the least of her problems. It was just so much in one day and so unlike the day before. I can think of only one other time when she had that gibberish speaking thing and within a day, she was back to normal. But today there were so many things!

Right away I think of a mistake in medication. No one mentions that, but we all know it happens.

Called Mom at 6:30. She had quite a spiel. She was going to bed. Had been watching a program I suggested, but *Louis couldn't get it on his TV*. She said it was hard to explain but *he cancelled something...* she did articulate words, but the thoughts were more like hallucinations. Maybe she had just talked to Louis, my uncle, on the phone. Anyway, the anxiety wasn't there and there were no physical complaints, but she didn't make sense. I told her it would be in the 80s tomorrow and I'd take her out for a ride, tomorrow is another day and all that. Goodnight and love ya.

APRIL 14, 2002

Mom called last night at 10:15 p.m. She was articulate but very confused. Said *she couldn't find, then where was*, something about *Nick*. Then but *where is Cate*? Something about someone going out East and *she hadn't discussed it* and she *felt so guilty*, etc. Uh-oh. This is not looking good.

I tried to call her from home about 6 a.m. No answer so I drove over. She was sitting in her chair fingering a pair of sunglasses. She said she was *trying to figure them out* and prattled on about a bunch of nonsense. Her words were clear but her thoughts weren't.

She talked about how she *enjoys smoking so much* and it *doesn't make her sick anymore*. Something about *maybe a hangover*. Then some more about how *if you don't have any money, people don't something...* Then that she had *to talk to Jenny about Louis. Had to do something for Louis* and how she gave him a list of chores and how he *just did them and how the goodness just came out of him*. I felt like I was watching a movie. This is Mom?

We sat in the sun for a while, then returned to her room. An aide said Mom had been walking outside her room without her walker or walking backwards with the walker- wanted to go upstairs because there was a box or a package she needed up there. Wow, this is bad. I wasn't ready for so rapid a deterioration.

And though her orientation may be abnormal because of Alzheimer's, she experiences normal emotions- fear and embarrassment- with no working cognitive tools with which to comfort herself. Such a cruel disease.

Don't have the lab results yet and it is Good Friday, so maybe nothing will happen until Monday or Tuesday on that front. Just need to help Mom—someone help me—through the weekend. Maybe I'll just let her talk and enter into the fray when she gets agitated to give her some comfort, otherwise just let her talk.

APRIL 15, 2002

Mom's labs were back today. Myra was there, told me they were normal. She said they would continue to observe her. Mom is coming out of her room without her walker; that suggests agitation but it's also normal to want to get out of the room. She was more herself today. She didn't even question going back to Riversite, not a peep. We had driven around, she went to the grocery story with me, got a coffee, no trouble holding or drinking it. Back at Riversite, watched a movie with her for a while. So I was relieved to have had such a normal visit. Don't know what happened the past three days or what they mean. Always suspicious of Riversite making a medication mistake. The incident is still a mystery.

But I do know a little about delirium. I did pay attention in class. Unlike dementia it comes on suddenly, but there are factors that contribute to it. Many elderly people in hospitals suffer from delirium. Sometimes urinary track infections cause it, but also changes in medication, sleep deprivation, etc., all of which happen in hospitals, and in nursing homes in Mom's case. Undoubtedly, her sleep has been disrupted and Blanche's medication has changed. Could a CNA have made a medication mistake? Or was Mom suffering from sleep deprivation?

Blanche was not up; she was in bed and sleeping when I left.

57

APRIL 17, 2002

Just checked in on Mom in morning, a little groggy, but not incoherent. Got her a coffee and turned on *Hello Dolly,* the movie version with Barbra Streisand. Mom's lip, according her CNA yesterday, was swollen. That swelling has happened in the past but not for a long time, and it was mostly gone today. Might be an allergic reaction. No one knows to what, though.

Blanche was not up; she was in bed and sleeping.

Back at Riversite, after an outing, Mom was confused about where she lives. An alarm signaled a tornado drill. Residents assembled in the hallway. Some could not be moved out of their rooms; staff just pulled a drape around them. That was Blanche's situation.

When I left, Blanche was uttering little "Help me's" but when I talked to her I don't think she even saw me, and I'm sure she didn't hear me. She looked like she had stopped breathing a few times but then started again. I alerted her CNA; she thought Blanche was upset because the curtain had been closed around her during the drill, but I had opened it. Anyway, Blanche looks like she has died already.

᠅᠅᠅᠅᠅᠅᠅᠅᠅᠅᠅᠅᠅᠅᠅᠅᠅᠅᠅᠅᠅

Today I had a care meeting with the social worker and nurse manager. Status quo with Mom and it seems Blanche has "rounded a corner." Yes, she lives and is taking up a great deal of space in the room and so is the aide who feeds her and moves the chairs around, plus opens Mom's curtains. I told the aide Mom likes them closed—Blanche used to as well before she became too ill to care—and I also mentioned it at the care meeting. People keep encroaching on Mom's little space. I mean it's only half of a room, smaller than a prison cell. Very frustrating.

The social worker said a room with a window side was available if we wanted to move Mom. Her roommate would be a German woman who is pretty confused and gets a lot of family company. The problem is she is in a wheelchair, too, and has a walker in her space. Mom would still have the obstacle course.

Later Mom complained about how they have set up Blanche right across the middle of the room in the big Broda chair. I asked Mom if she would like to move to a different room. I told her I could arrange it for her.

She said, "No. It might be worse." She's right.

APRIL 20, 2002

Met Mom coming down the hall after lunch.

"What brings you here?" she asked, smiling brightly.

"You," I answered.

All in all, it was reassuring to have Mom seeming more herself today.

Blanche was up in her giant chair, feet sticking out into Mom's passing area. I could have moved her chair back a bit, but her oxygen machine was in the way.

❧❧❧❧❧❧❧❧❧❧❧❧❧❧❧❧❧❧❧❧

I called Mom about 6:45p.m. with movie advice. She was thinking about putting on her pjs. She left the phone to turn on her TV and came back to the phone confused. Finally, she located her remote and pressed the power button. The TV was absolutely blaring. Someone had probably turned it up for Mom to hear over the din of Blanche's protestations. It took about 10 more minutes to coach her through volume control. She was agitated by the time we got that far, but she was successful.

APRIL 27, 2002

Drove Mom through a local park, then back to Riversite. Got her a coffee and straightened out her room.

Blanche was wailing, "Help me, help me." I went to her bedside and she said she wanted to go to bed. I pressed her nurse button twice. Two different aides came in. She told each one she wanted to go to bed. Each one told her she was already in bed. One aide just told her; the other barked. You could not call that consolation.

Mom said Blanche does that all the time as though it doesn't alarm her anymore; I hope it doesn't.

ॐ॰ॐ॰ॐ॰ॐ॰ॐ॰ॐ॰ॐ॰ॐ॰ॐ॰ॐ॰ॐ॰ॐ॰ॐ॰ॐ॰ॐ॰ॐ॰ॐ॰ॐ

Called Mom at 6:15 p.m.; she was in bed, persuaded her to get up and to turn on a movie, *The Sting*. Called again at 7 p.m.; she was in bed again and didn't want to get up. "I'm tired." I went over the events of the past two days to suggest why she might have fatigue; she said it all sounded quite eventful and she wished she could remember it all. "I do remember having a good time, though." This is a refrain of hers. To me it means she still enjoys life.

MAY 4, 2002

Mom was good today- has been past week. Blanche was down in bed today, but up and perky two days ago.

MAY 5, 2002

Blanche's niece was there, concerned about Blanche's pain. She said hospice ordered her to have morphine as needed. So we discussed who decides when it's needed. Blanche doesn't even remember she has a nurse call button sometimes, maybe doesn't understand she can request morphine. Then the niece said, "You think they would be checking in periodically to see if Blanche is in pain." Sophia said that because she thinks they aren't.

⋘⋘⋘⋘⋘⋘⋘⋘⋘⋘⋘⋘⋘⋘⋘⋘⋘⋘⋘⋘

You'd think, that assumption, the expectation of a vigil...when I was in high school, a sophomore isolated himself in small study alcove of the library, became bored and decided it might be fun to climb atop a table, remove a ceiling tile and hoist himself into world above. He crawled around above the library until a tile gave way. The lower half of his body hatched out of the ceiling to the glee and applause of students below. I thought it was the most magnificent feat I had ever seen. The principal called the boy's father who charged into the library indignantly complaining that the school had failed to properly supervise his son. I could feel his pain, in a way. He was embarrassed and frustrated; just assumed his son would be safe if he were in school. But kids are not under the direct gaze of school employees at all times and in all places. That would be impossible. Sometimes I read in a newspaper about a patient at a mental health facility or hospital who hangs himself or escapes some other way. Expressions like these, *he was not getting proper care or supervision...family is tormented that such misfortune could occur while under the care of medical professionals*, suggest that when people deposit a loved one at an institution, they believe the attention he gets will be constant. Vigil and vigilance? At nursing homes, the professionals who work most directly with residents, certified nursing assistants like me, are not at the bedside throughout. They serve multiple residents with multiple needs. Sophia knows her aunt isn't being monitored as much as she would like. And that's a painful reality. I'm dreading the day when I have to watch Mom go through this. I don't want aides to be dispassionate toward her. But I know that can happen.

Now Blanche always wants to go back to bed; then when she's in bed, she asks to be put in bed. Down to 74 pounds. Don't get how she can stand it. Every movement hurts. Poor Blanche. What a way to go.

Blanche had labored breathing and was unresponsive in the afternoon. She is expected to die soon. I don't believe it, though. She was really feisty this morning.

MAY 13, 2002

Blanche's side of the room had been stripped before I arrived. An aide said she died yesterday about 5 p.m. The staff had seen from the pallor, shallow and labored breathing and unresponsiveness that Blanche would expire soon. They called Sophia who was able to be with her when she died.

Mom was sitting in her recliner looking through a box of old family photos again. She said, "I'm trying to find my future." Did she say future but mean past? Or did she think there was some clue to her future by looking to the past?

I didn't talk to Mom about the death although she did stop to look at Blanche's bed when we walked in from lunch. I don't know how she understands this, but I do know she is afraid of dying so I don't bring it up.

MAY 14, 2002

In the evening I called Mom. She said Blanche hadn't been in all day. I told her she may have gone to the hospital; she was pretty sick. She said the place was topsy turvy but "they did a good job." I think the room must have been cleaned out and disinfected. Mom seemed unaffected, though, and was ready to watch a Robert Mitchum movie.

∽∾∽∾∽∾∽∾∽∾∽∾∽∾∽∾∽∾∽∾∽

But at 2 a.m., my phone rang, Mom in an agitated state, disoriented about where she was, wanted me to call her father (deceased 26 years) to let him know where she was... I told her I would be coming over later and she wanted specifics about later. That is what she wanted, someone to come over. She may have awakened to find herself alone in a room that had previously contained Blanche. Maybe she understood that Blanche had died. Maybe staff told her. No way to know. I reassured her I would be over later in the day. She said, "Don't let me down." She seemed a little calmer and did not call back. I will see her later today and she won't remember this. I'm not sure how to handle the Blanche story and I don't think it will be long before Riversite puts someone else in Mom's room- another hurdle.

CHAPTER SIX

Journeys
Sophia's Nightmare
By Cate

I wrote to Sophia a month after her aunt Blanche died. After seeing Blanche's obituary, "Blanche Dubois died May 12, age 96. Private services were held," I thought Sophia would appreciate hearing from me.

Dear Sophia,

I had the pleasure of getting to know your aunt when I was visiting Mom. She was a sweet lady. Hope you don't mind my having tooled an obituary from my point of view:

Blanche Dubois is survived by her niece Sophia who loved her and didn't forget her like her other nieces and nephews did. Blanche resided in a nursing home for her final eight years and kept my mother Jessie company for four of those. Blanche had no teeth or dentures, but she could smile sweetly with her eyes and she did when she said, "My niece brings me roses because she knows I love them... She brings me strawberry pie because she knows it is my favorite... She brought me these fleecy slipper boots because she wants me to be comfortable." Even when Sophia wasn't there, pleasant thoughts of her sustained Blanche.

Sophia wrote back, said the thoughts meant a lot to her. She said before Blanche died she was frightened by talk she heard of another resident's death. After a nursing home resident dies, family is expected to claim the resident's possessions. On Blanche and Jessie's unit earlier this year, a female resident died, and no one came to claim her possessions or her body. News of that travesty spread among other residents like gossip in a school hallway. The residents on first floor were shaken. None of them wants to end that way. And Blanche, according to Sophia, was like the others, frightened.

Then she shared, in her journal, what happened the day after Blanche died when she returned to Riversite to pick up Blanche's things.

...after I gathered together Blanche's spare belongings, I dropped, emotionally empty, into a chair next to her stripped bed. Mechanically, I turned on her small TV. It was a weather report, and it transported me to an earlier time, 15 years ago, a hot, humid summer day. The weather forecaster then advised families to check up on seniors living alone. My husband and I knew Blanche's solo living arrangement, but at age 80, she might have trouble tolerating heat. She had no car, never learned to drive, no phone. Only way to check on her was to drive there. There she was in stifling heat, sitting in front of a small fan that served only to move heat around, not to cool it. Seeing Blanche like that, I resolved to somehow get her back in the family. I included her in family gatherings, picked her up for Thanksgiving and Christmas, mixed her up with cousins, nieces, nephews, made her less isolated. But, as is often the case, as you and I have discussed, Cate, one person assumes primary care responsibility, and it was I. Blanche's health declined in 1994, and when she could no longer care for herself, I made arrangements for her admission to Riversite.

I was exhausted by the whole ordeal that ended with Blanche's death, but there was still the memorial service to arrange. Then I made the calls.

A cousin: "She didn't have much of a life anyway."

A niece: "I'd like to come, but I have already made plans."

A nephew: "I wish I had visited Blanche more, but I just hate nursing homes."

A cousin: I used to feel bad about Blanche all alone, but at some point, a person just has to move on.

A former neighbor: "I'd come to the funeral, but I won't know anyone there but you."

A former employer: "Well, um, I guess she died like she lived- alone."

None of the people I called attended. But I know I'll hear from them soon.

I didn't know what she meant by that last remark until I got her Christmas card and the attached letter.

Dear Cate,

Hope you and your mother are well enough.... I have finally gotten those calls I told you would come.

After Blanche died, her attorney contacted me. Turns out Blanche had an attorney and for years, an accountant. The many years lived so frugally were not spent squandering her few resources. Her own parents had left her holdings in several prosperous companies. She never cashed them in, just kept an eye on them and kept quiet about them. And that started when she was 20. She died at 96 so her money had 76 years to grow. I knew she had savings, enough to pay for her care at Riversite, but she said it might run out if she secured a private room. I did not know what she had.

After my husband and I rescued Blanche that hot day in Milwaukee, I became, as far as she was concerned, the lawyer said, heir to receive her trust. She never shared knowledge of her accumulated wealth to anyone, not even me. But it is in the millions.

There was no joy in this inheritance. I am more angry than grateful. I suppose she didn't know the extent to which I agonized about her, wished I could have garnered more family support for her, gotten Riversite to provide more comfort, compassion in her declining years. I hope this doesn't offend you as a nursing home caregiver, but from what I observed, most residents just lie on their beds or sit in their chairs, for hours and hours and hours and no one talks to them. Most don't have phones. They are "housed" like dogs in a kennel. Oh, I know that's a terrible thing to say, but that's what I think now. People feed them, give them their meds, bath them, you know, the basics, keep them safe. But that is not enough. People who think they have enough if they have enough money for a nursing home just don't know. The institution isn't enough. Who provides the caring, the quality of life?

Money can't buy happiness but it sure does enhance options. Blanche's money could have meant a first rate nursing home, a private room. Or if Blanche preferred, a senior residence and home care with private doctors and nurses, round the clock; the money was there. At the very least, had I known, I would have asked her to let me direct her care. I could have hired private caregivers to assist Blanche on the days I couldn't see her myself. Someone to drive her around on a sunny day, like you do for your mother sometimes. Those lonely days when no one spoke to Blanche? I would have paid people to provide companionship. My head is swimming with ways I could have used that money to help her. Yes, I have a huge inheritance now, don't even have to work anymore, but no living Blanche to thank, no peace of mind when I recall her last lonely days, and a bunch of relatives calling both me and Blanche's lawyer to see what stake they might claim.

I'm not offended by Sophia's caregiver remarks. She was speaking out of grief and pain, and she's right about some things. Just being in a nursing home is not care enough. But all that business about money to enhance Blanche's care—my belief is if people looking for volunteer work could shake off the *oh, I just hate going into a nursing home* excuse, nursing home residents would be the happy recipients of much more personal attention. All nursing homes need more volunteers, and a big volunteer force can be the difference between a "happy home" and a sad one. I'm sorry Sophia feels angry at Blanche, though. Blanche probably was so accustomed to not spending money on herself, she just didn't know how. Maybe she didn't see the anguish her last days caused her niece. Or maybe she was a fiery independent spirit. When people with cognitive disabilities like Mom's or physical disabilities like Blanche's wind up institutionalized, they have already suffered a series of affronts to their independence. First their car keys are taken away. Then they are yanked from their homes. Then they lose their privacy, can't even handle toilet paper privately. But good for Blanche who didn't lose it all. She hung on to one of her most private parts, her net worth.

CHAPTER SEVEN

Endings
Jimmy: The End of the Road
By Billie

Mum could, in 2001, remember her WWII youth as a girl living in Kettering, Scotland, and Corby, England. She remembered American GIs in town, dance bands, air raid sirens, her father taking her and her siblings to a bomb shelter in the back yard, and a stray bomb hitting the post office where she worked when she was 18. Those memories are 60-70 years old. People with Alzheimer's retain those older memories and lose the most recent ones first. Eventually, Mum will remember nothing. Now, just two years after her Alzheimer's diagnosis, she doesn't remember major life events of 40-50 years ago.

For starters, Mum has forgotten that her son, my brother, died. The first time Mum asked me if I ever see my brother, I said, "You mean *your* brother Jackson?"

She pointed to the framed picture behind me. My brother Jimmy, arms outstretched and surrounded by pigeons, is standing in front of Buckingham Palace in London.

"No, *your* brother Jimmy," she answered.

I tried to jog her memory with old letters written by her mother and sister and other family who lived in England at the time my brother Jimmy died. Mum had taken him to England in 1958 to attend her brother Jackson's wedding, meet relatives and see the sights of London. But Mum couldn't remember this. Jimmy met his British side of the family for the first (and last) time. Less than a year later, he complained of fatigue. Doctors tentatively diagnosed mononucleosis, then following more tests, changed that to leukemia, an acute and fatal form. I read these letters to Mum:

MAY 13, 1959

Dear Joan and Lincoln,

I still don't know quite what to say to you. It has all been so sudden.....all my memories of Jimmy raise a smile. I think he had a very happy life and that is something to be glad of... Your son made a lot of friends when he was over here... we too feel that we have lost someone dear to us.

Love, Mary [Mum's sister]

MAY 14, 1959

Dear Lincoln and Joan,

I feel I must write to you and convey to you our sorrow on your sad bereavement; it is indeed a tragic loss...words cannot express how shocked we were to hear such distressing news...it is my hope that you will regain tranquility of mind and courage to endure. I know that I am expressing the feelings of all your kinsfolk in Scotland and elsewhere and that they all join with me in hoping that the future years will be kind to you.

Our warmest affect,

Aunt Jean, Uncle Liam and Laurie

And some of the daily letters from Mum's mother:

MAY 11, 1959

...I just don't know how to tell you how sorry we are about Jimmy. I just can't believe it, Joan.

MAY 12, 1959

Dear Joan and Lincoln,

...I hope you are feeling a wee bit better today, just take each day as it comes Joan and you will be surprised how you will get through.

MAY 13, 1959

My first thought was to come over and try to help you but I find I cannot manage it.
Love,
Mum

Mum's face tightened, distress over not remembering. "What happened?" Then I told Mum the rest of the story, at least as my memory serves.

Jimmy had been hospitalized for about seven days. That week Dad took my sister and me with him to the hospital after he finished work. Mum was already there. We had to bring our homework. There was a hospital rule that children under a certain age, 12 I think, could not visit patients, so we didn't actually see Jimmy. I thought—because this is what Dad told us—that Jimmy had pneumonia. That didn't strike me as particularly frightening.

I had walked from home about three blocks to a local store, Brown's News Stand, in Lake Foxbrook where the clerk knew me and my family. I had my pet crow Joe on my shoulder and my English Setter Feller in tow—both tolerated by the locals. The store clerk asked me how Jimmy was. I said he was getting better. The clerk looked very concerned.

He said, "What is wrong with Jimmy?"

I said, "He has pneumonia." The clerk's face went stony. I felt very uncomfortable.

Later, on the way into the hospital, I asked, "Dad, people don't die of pneumonia, do they?"

His face was a rock like the clerk's. He said, "You can die of anything if you have it bad enough." He spoke those words into space.

I knew Jimmy would die.

I think Mum and Dad must have been overwhelmed, or maybe my uncle just wanted to help in some way. The last few days Jimmy was alive, Anne and I stayed with my Uncle Lance and Aunt Daisy at their house in Chicago; it was somebody's idea but it wasn't ours.

Of that week I recall spending a lot of time in Uncle Lance and Aunt Daisy's TV room doing homework. Aunt Daisy suggested we attend school in Chicago while we were there; we must have been getting on her nerves. I took part of a sandwich out of the refrigerator to eat and she scolded me because that was supposed to be Uncle Lance's lunch the next day. My older cousin Carol threatened to wash my mouth out with soap for saying *shit*. In 2004 (43 years later), I ran into that cousin at a family reunion. The first thing she said to me was,

"Billie, I remember telling you I was going to wash your mouth out with soap for swearing."

I said, "Yes, I remember. I said shit," and thought in my own family, I never worried about my mouth being washed out with anything. If I said *shit* at home, I might have to put 25 cents of my allowance money in the swears jar, which profited most by my father's many *damn its*. As a matter of fact, I don't recall any mistreatment although I did get spanked a few times with the back of the hair brush for my most serious transgression: saying the *F* word. I first heard it in Milwaukee when we lived on the south side. I didn't know what it meant, but I said it once at home and the brush came out. Then I knew it was truly evil and it possessed me for a while. I would go to bed and say my prayers and the *F* word would compulsively appear in my thoughts. Finally, I asked God for forgiveness and all of a sudden I was thinking, "*F@#** you, God!" and to my great amazement, God did not smite me. Then I knew it was true that God loves all his children and the F word demon in me was exorcized.

Anyway, I would like to have told my cousin how full of shit she was but I had no courage at the moment, plus I knew she had been married and divorced three times (thrice dumped probably) and her daughter had died at age 32 of a heart attack related to diabetes. Probably the bully had already been beaten out of her.

Back in 1959 my aunt told us Jimmy passed away and we would be going home. I had never been to a funeral, and I was afraid to go to this one.

Years later, Mum had therapy when we lived in Barrington, as part of treatment for depression. I attended a few sessions with her therapist, who told me privately she could tell from my choice of words that I had come from a family with a lot of sickness. I used expressions like, *It made me sick, I almost died*, etc. She thought those early experiences helped mold that part of me which is a caretaker personality.

The therapist's observation about sickness was accurate. My sister had convulsions as a baby and into her early childhood; she sometimes had seizures at night. Doctors thought it might have been a form of neurological polio; it began right at the end of the polio epidemic. I tried to wake Anne in her crib one morning and wondered how she could be asleep and awake at the same time.

My mother called up the stairs, "Billie, get Anne out of bed."

I called back, "She's sleeping with her eyes open!"

Things happened very quickly then. I watched from the porch as Mum and Dad flew frantically out the front door to the car with Anne in Mum's arms. At the hospital, I was to learn, doctors said they could do nothing for Anne, that night convulsions and a comatose state could recur, especially if she developed fever. They prescribed a very mild sedative for nighttime. She took this until she was 14 years old when another doctor told my mother that the amount was appropriate for an infant and so miniscule that she may as well have been taking nothing at all, so it was discontinued. She, in fact, didn't need it. Those scary spells stopped occurring after Anne entered the early grades of elementary school, but the worry that my parents experienced didn't. Whenever Anne was sick there was fear. Mum was afraid even when Anne became emotional. So she told me not to cry at Jimmy's funeral to protect Anne. Maybe that's why I was so afraid to go. Do not cry at your brother's funeral—what a big order!

I didn't want to go, but Mum bought me a new dress and told me I had to attend. A new dress, people bringing food to the house, a lot of company. Seemed awfully important. Don't cry. More pressure.

Then the funeral. When I saw my brother in the casket, I burst into noisy tears. He didn't look "passed away," "gone to heaven," or "at peace." He looked plain old dead and he didn't look like Jimmy. Jimmy had a crew cut but now his hair was parted and slicked down to the sides. His freckled face seemed flat and, well, lifeless.

Music played in the background, a recorded song, with lyrics like *...reaching the end of my road.* A peculiar choice for the death of a 12-year-old.

Mum's brother, the only relative from her side of the family at the funeral, sat in the row in front of me next to my parents; I, blubbering away, sat with Anne and started her crying. Uncle Jackson turned around and handed me one of his handkerchiefs. Mum and Dad, sitting in front of us, made no sounds or movements, making me feel all the more conspicuous doing all that crying, but it was truly beyond my control. My recall is that no one else cried. At a funeral of a young child, that cannot be possible. I believe my self-consciousness thundered so loudly in my 10-year-old head that I couldn't hear others.

We filed into cars for the trip to the burial site, a little cemetery on top of a hill; I thought it was like Boot Hill on *Gunsmoke* and said so. My uncle liked that. It was a foil to the somberness of the occasion. Mum said she remembers the cemetery but not the people in attendance. I asked her if she remembered Clint. She said, "I can't picture him but I think I never liked him."

So I told her a few things about my cousin Clint. He didn't think I seemed sad enough. I told him what a well meaning but inept relative had just told me- that whenever someone dies, a baby is born in the world. That's not sad. He said, "Wouldn't you rather have your brother than some baby you don't even know?" Ouch. Truth hurts. Clint was right. I didn't care about the foreign baby. But Clint didn't have to say that. He lacked empathy which explains his dearth of friends.

And as if things weren't bad enough, Clint stayed with us for at least a week after Jimmy died. His father Louis, Mum's favorite brother-in-law, thought it would be good for my dad to have Clint around and that Clint might somehow benefit. I don't know where he got this idea. And both Louis and my father are dead, so I can't find out. Clint was 14, got into fights, was a loner and rocked in his bed at night, an injured psyche trying to comfort itself. To simplify, he had demons. By day, though, he was the big white hunter and he liked to kill animals. My dog Acey barked incessantly and scared away birds that Clint enjoyed shooting, so he took a shot at my dog with his pellet gun. I told my parents and Clint was gone.

At the 2004 family reunion in Hodag, Clint heard lots of stories about himself from relatives who couldn't wait to tell him. "You know what a family reunion is to me?" he asked. "A chance for people to tell me all the things I did that were wrong." He remembered that he had stayed at our house, but he said he couldn't remember why he left. I could have told him, but I have a hard time beating up people who have already been pulverized.

Clint's father Louis never told him he was adopted. When he joined the Navy, an enlistment officer identified his real father. That shook Clint's world. There is a story that he was engaged to be married but he stood up his bride and instead headed to Alaska for an extended fishing/hunting trip. The trip lasted 40 plus years, and that isn't just family lore. For 17 of those years, Clint trapped and hunted in the Arctic wilderness and ran from his demons. He traded with residents of an Inuit village. A modern day Jeremiah Johnson. Then he "settled down" and married an Eskimo woman and had two sons. He got a "real" job working in a copper mine within the Arctic Circle where he still works today. Louis never gave up on him. I think he was the only one in the family who still liked Clint. He called Clint, in the mines, on his 50th birthday and told him he was as proud of him then as he was on the day he adopted him. Clint said he cried on the spot.

Clint tells me he's born again and is trying to do a lot of good deeds to make up for all the bad ones of his rather tormented past. I think evangelical Christianity and Clint are a good match. Clint's okay now. I like him, too.

∛∛∛∛∛∛∛∛∛∛∛∛

My brother's gravestone says *Our Son Jimmy 1947-1959.* I thought the tombstone should have said and *Brother to Anne and Billie.* No point in discussing that with my mother now. I took Mum to Lake Foxbrook to visit the grave once after her Alzheimer's diagnosis and reprise the story of how she drove up from Florida in 1990 with Dad's ashes and sprinkled them on Jimmy's grave. Dad would have liked that. In Hodag, he was a policeman who didn't practice what he preached. For one thing, he shot a deer while on duty and stuffed the carcass into his squad car, back seat. The deer, stunned rather than dead, kicked the inside of the squad to shreds. He fished more than once with three lines instead of the legal one line. When confronted and questioned, he said, "I wasn't catching anything with one." He got caught. *Never got away with anything,* he would say. I told Mum that Dad would have liked his ashes sprinkled on Jimmy's grave because it was an illegal act, and in the end he got away with something.

My sister and I should have been with our mother when she dispersed those ashes, though. Why she didn't include us, I don't know. She said, at the time, it was hard, but she needed to do it by herself. Now she doesn't remember.

One theory about the cause of dementia is excessive stress hormones, over a long period of time. Six months after Jimmy died, Mum had a nervous breakdown which hospitalized her. She was prone to episodes of depression and anxiety the rest of her adult life, tending always to route stress inward instead of outward. I don't know if anxiety and depression played a role in her Alzheimer's development, so much is not known.

After I explained the events surrounding Jimmy's death, Mum said quietly, "Well, I guess that's life. And I don't remember it." I told her it is not a happy memory. Actually, that bit of history is—there's that word again—shit, so maybe forgetting isn't all bad. She looked worried so I changed the subject. I have learned to deflect her anxiety by distraction or if that doesn't work, by climbing into her world with her...

On Oct. 30 (Halloween) Mum knocked on my bedroom door at 5 a.m. She said she just got back from vacation. I told her it was 5 a.m. and she said, "Yes, I just got up." I urged her to go back to bed, but she didn't hear a word I said. What was on her mind was Ian. "I don't think I have Ian's phone number," she said. I knew it was there, next to her phone, and she'd be using it to wake him next. She made her call to Ian.

About 6:30, another knock at my bedroom door. Breathlessness, the sound of anxiety, upset because he had gone to the lake and she was worried. I asked her who he was and, after a lot of muttering, she said, "Your brother."

"Mum, you mean your brother Jackson?"

"No, no. Jimmy, my boy. You were there."

"Where, Mum?"

"Here. He was here in this house with six boys and they went to the lake. He's been gone so long; he knows I'm worried."

"What lake, Mum? Do you mean Lake Foxbrook ?"

"No, not Lake Foxbrook ."

"Do you mean Lake Michigan?"

"No."

"Is the lake in Florida?"

"Yes, it's in Florida."

"Okay, Mum, I'm packing right now. I'll go to Florida. I'll go find him and bring him back. I'll be able to find him, okay?"

"Oh, thank you. Oh, oh, I hope so."

"Don't worry, Mum."

"I can't help it."

I got up, got dressed. Let her see me get my car keys and walk into the garage. She went back to her room. That's how it went. Current thinking is that trying to reason with an Alzheimer's patient who is obviously confused or delusional is counterproductive. Try to enter into that patient's present world, even if you have to tell little white lies; he or she isn't going to remember anyway. Also, don't bring it up later which would embarrass the person. Unfortunately, I hear well-meaning people doing just that. I think I have done it, too. Not anymore.

I could not divert Mum from her lost Jimmy mindset until I entered into the dialog and assured her that I would find him. I knocked on her bedroom door fifteen minutes later and she seemed calm; there was no mention of Jimmy.

What may have been the catalyst for this delusion was Halloween, groups of children trick or treating in the neighborhood. Mum had seen little boys on the porch. A little boy who looked like Jimmy or whose name was Jimmy may have impressed her. That's just my guess.

CHAPTER EIGHT

Endings
Riversite Healthcare Center and John: The End of the Road
By Cate

I f you happen upon the east end of the first floor of Riversite about 12:15 p.m. on a typical day, you might mistake it for a Karaoke party. A white haired 80-year-old is mouthing the lyrics to the BeeGees' song *Staying Alive, "...Life goin' nowhere. Somebody help me...yeah. I'm stayin' alive...,"* and working hard at gyrations as he closes his eyes and imagines himself starring in *Saturday Night Fever.* But what the residents see is an old guy jerking to the left and then jerking to the right, movements limited by knee and hip replacements. It is John, but not John Travolta.

And it's not a party. It's the dining room on Mom's floor. Set up like a restaurant, multiple tables for four, white linen table cloths, lots of windows and a stone fireplace at one end, the space is actually quite inviting. During lunch, the big meal of the day, aides set up each resident with juice, milk, decaf coffee, and food designed to meet their individual nutritional needs. John assists the dining room staff (as a volunteer) by helping get residents into the dining room, setting tables, pouring coffee, collecting bibs afterwards, wheeling residents back to their rooms, etc.

Residents needing assistance to eat are clustered together at one end of the room to make best use of the aides. Independent eaters gather around tables at the fireplace end. Mum is at the table directly in front of the fireplace. Two of her tablemates are a married couple, John the crooner, who comes to Riversite each day from about 8:30 a.m. to 2 p.m., and his wife, Dee, a resident. He is mentally sharp but hard of hearing and walking stiffly from those joint replacements. Dee's Alzheimer's has degraded her language significantly. She speaks mainly gibberish, is sometimes very pleasant and smiley and other times irritable and uncooperative.

John lives by himself in a village of apartments for seniors, close to Riversite. A very bright man, and former engineer, he used to work on American submarines and aircraft carriers designing ways to eliminate asbestos in construction, claiming the asbestos killed soldiers, among them his own brother. He also worked in Alaska designing ways to extract iron from mines. "My wife's people are from up there," he said. "That's where I met her." What might have been a happy retirement at "the lake house" had to be exchanged for cash. He had to sell their lake property to accommodate her care. Then she broke both her knees and ankles in falls, so a walker has become an attachment and movement with that requires assistance.

Somehow, he finds energy to croon to tunes during the dinner hour. Undoubtedly, he's frustrated by lack of mental stimulation in his current situation. His wife can't participate in dialogue. When he spoke of Alaska, he mentioned Ketchikan. I told him I learned during an Alaskan cruise of the Inside Passage about the prostitution history there, that the downtown was comprised of whorehouses. He said, "Oh, yes, I took a peek in there." Dee's ears perk up when he gets going like that but I'm not sure how she encodes what he says. She tries to break in sometimes. I think it's a scolding. She might say, "You are

85

going to be a beggar for 120 years," or, "Put the heat nowhere thing back there," or "Drop dead."

After lunch one typical day, I ran into John in the hallway just outside his wife's room. He told me he asked Jessie if he could call her honey and she said, "Sure." Then he asked her if she knew what honey was. He told her, "It's bee shit!" Then he said, "Bye, honeybee." Gleefully. John likes to push the envelope, as the expression goes, right to the edge and then pull himself back, just before he is in trouble.

He reminded me, "I think I offended you the other day when I asked you what was under your shirt."

"I knew you were just teasing."

"But what if I had said, 'Show me your cleavage'?"

"That would be crossing a line."

He said, "But why? On TV all the girls show cleavage, even the news broadcasters. I don't mind it though. Sometimes I think I'm dead and then I see that and I feel my heart start beating again." This is why I call him JohnJuanawoman.

His shenanigans try my patience occasionally, but he makes Mom laugh and he tries to keep her out of harm's way. I may work at Riversite, but I can't oversee Mom all the time; I have to be careful that my attention to her is on my own time, not when I'm on the clock. I'm not on her unit, and I know the aides are often overwhelmed with their duties, so having John present during the noon meal is a comfort to me. When Mom leaves the dining room without her walker, he stops her. If she doesn't show up for lunch, he walks to her room, wakes her if she is sleeping, and makes sure she uses her walker. He knows he's not supposed to do that, enter a resident's room, but he does. He sees a need and that's what he responds to, doesn't care what the rules are. CNAs are trained not to force residents; at the same time, they know the health value of getting residents moving, sitting up and socializing. If Mom refuses to go to lunch, staff would bring her lunch on a tray, she wouldn't starve, but she'd eat in isolation; that is not what she needs. The carrot John dangles before her is the promise of two cups of coffee in the dining room, with cream and sugar. That usually gets her there.

One day she sneezed and her dentures flew out, landing on the floor. Mom would eventually have picked them up, probably wiped them on her bib and as discreetly as she could, put them unhygienically back in her mouth. The aides may have retrieved the dentures if they'd noticed they weren't in Jessie's mouth, but they are so busy helping residents eat, they probably hadn't seen the airborne choppers. John picked up the dentures, took them to the sink, washed them and gave them back to Mom.

Another day, a wintry one, he gave me and Mom a weather and driving report, advising us not to venture out. He'd had an accident; his car slid into a guard rail. I took his advice and Mom and I stayed in.

A few days later, Jan. 1, John approached me as Mom and I signed out for an afternoon, my day off. He said "Happy New Year," and came in close for a kiss. I turned my head in an avoidance maneuver. One of the nurses whispered to me, "If Dee had seen him do that, she would really have been mad." I'd witnessed some of Dee's rages. One day just after Christmas, I joined the lunch table, John assisting Mom with her food as usual, getting her second and third cups of coffee, Dee contentedly concentrating on her food, using her fingers to eat these days. John asked me if I liked Dee's new Christmas blouse. I admired it and

Dee turned her head toward me and responded with gibberish, "That has been in the barn. For 120 years you and your mother!" Then John smiled at her. She turned toward him and clearly enunciated, "You shut your face! Shut it!"

A nurse said that a few years ago when she was new and didn't know Dee yet, she tried to engage her as John signed her out. The nurse said, "Have a good time, Dee."

Dee scowled at the nurse and said, "He thinks he's going to get some." This nurse and others, including me, have marveled at the need to "learn" each resident.

This year, John stopped taking Dee out. She is incontinent, her walking unstable and her behavior erratic. Dee's advancing dementia qualifies her for a move to third floor where most of the dementia patients are clustered, but John insists that she stays where she is. He's afraid of the upstairs wing because the perception is people are sicker up there. Maybe he thinks if he keeps Dee on this floor, she won't degrade to the next stage of Alzheimer's.

After lunch, when the dining room had emptied, he sits close to his wife, his head in his hands, weary. I never see his (their) children visit. The burden of Dee is all his. I can see her lips moving, and I know she is probably not making sense. Maybe he just likes to hear her voice or maybe, as I have noticed, once in a while she makes sense. I can never tell what Dee is thinking, but if she ever worries about losing her husband, she doesn't need to. It is the other way around. The same principal is true of Jessie. She's not losing me; I'm losing her.

When Mom was admitted to Riversite, she could walk without the walker and was less confused but very bored. There was a 40-50ish, young for a resident, wheelchair-bound woman at her table,

Kathy. She was loud and obnoxious, always trying to get someone to go out and buy her cigarettes and then later accusing the person of not giving her the change, etc. Her caregivers had trouble modifying her behavior. I told Jessie it was too bad that woman had to be at her table, but Jessie said she liked Kathy because unlike others, Kathy talked a lot, added levity. John appreciated her, too.

"At least she's not a deadbeat!" A deadbeat to John was someone who stared into space and didn't talk. Nursing homes have a lot of those.

He liked lively people, even if they were unorthodox. A great audience for someone who performed as long as the performance was stimulating, i.e. witty, John could take over the show himself. Riversite schedules regular afternoon activities, sometimes bringing in musicians who begin their acts with one-liners. If the jokes fell flat, John volunteered to tell a few. The man could not be intimidated or embarrassed. And he had a keen eye for spotting a fake. He especially couldn't stand married couples who seemed idyllic. He'd say, "Show me the perfect couple and I'll show you at least one liar!" Undoubtedly, his own marriage was flawed.

Once during those early Riversite days, John spotted a distraught looking Kathy moping in her wheelchair as she sat in a courtyard outside the dining room puffing on a cigarette. John left his table, peered through the window, interested. She should have been at the table by now. The most direct route to Kathy was through the door marked emergency exit only. An alarm sounded and dining room aides glared as he pushed his way through.

"What wrong, Kathy?"

As John bent down to hear her answer, and bending wasn't easy for him, Kathy-the-loudmouth barely whispered, as if confessing, "My father put his finger in my vagina." Oh no. What will John say to that? I feared for Kathy. But he leaned into the woman's face and whispered back, gently, "That wasn't your fault. You don't have to feel bad about that. That was not your fault." The woman stopped crying and her face relaxed. I was in awe of Johnjuanawoman. He wheeled Kathy back in through the emergency door, the alarm sounded again. Then he deposited Kathy at her proper place next to his wife. It was a rather magnanimous moment.

So I don't fault the people at that table.

Unfortunately, Mom no longer dines with Dee and John. I was wrong when I said Dee didn't have to worry about losing him. Noticing John's absence a few consecutive days and Dee in a wheelchair instead of using her walker—John insisted she use her walker rather than capitulate to a wheelchair—I asked an aide if he had taken a vacation. The aide said John was in a hospital, not sure for what reason, but serious and needing surgery. To my knowledge, he never came back.

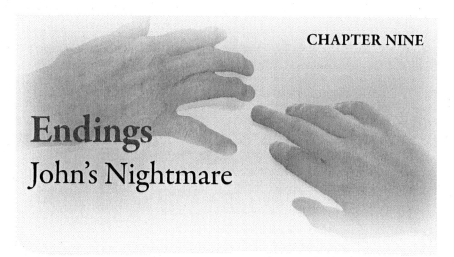

CHAPTER NINE

Endings
John's Nightmare

The scene: *John is phoning his wife Dee. He makes this call, even now that he is hospitalized, between 6:30 and 7 p.m. the past three evenings to guide Dee's TV selections. Dee cannot follow a TV guide, too confusing. But if she doesn't get a movie on her TV, she goes to bed early and is up pacing in the middle of the night, sometimes in her room, sometimes in the hallway of her Riversite unit. Night time pacing/wandering is common among people with Alzheimer's. But John believes if his wife would just stay up longer, she'd sleep through the night. He coaches Dee.*

John: "Dee, there's a good movie on Channel 58."

Dee: "When?"

John: "Now."

Dee: "What country?"

John has learned that the correct response to that question is, "Turn on the TV, then come back to the phone." Otherwise, Dee goes to the TV, presses the power button and then looks for a way to change the channel on the television set. She never made the leap to remote. If she is frustrated, she turns the TV off and goes to bed.

Dee, *returning to the phone*: "What?"

John: "Go to your TV, turn it on."

Dee: "On the what?"

John is accustomed to Dee's inability to use language correctly and to focus on directions that require more than one step.

John: "Just turn it on and then come back to the phone."

John waits and hopes that Dee hasn't forgotten her mission.

Dee returns to the phone: "Hello?"

John: "Yes."

Dee: "*Now?*"

John: "Now you need to get your hand-held remote. It's a gray object that looks like a thin phone."

Dee: "Don't know that. The phone?"

John, *patient but insistent*: "It is usually on one of your table tops, usually the table next to your recliner."

Dee: "What? Wait."

John patiently waits and hopes Dee hasn't been distracted by something.

Dee: "Sony."

John: "That's it! Now, do you have your glasses on?"

Dee: "No."

John patiently waits.

Dee, *putting on her glasses*: "Okay?"

John: "Do you see the numbers on your Sony?"

Dee: "Uh huh."

John: "Okay, first press the five, then the eight."

Dee: "Eight?"

John: "First five, then eight."

Dee, *begins her task and mouths the first number*: " Fiiiive."

John: "And then eight. Five and then eight."

Dee: "Five....and then eight. Eight. Nine. Ten."

John: "What's on now?"

Dee: "TV."

John: "I mean describe what is on the television screen."

Dee: "No."

John: "Is the TV turned on?"

Dee puts down the remote, wobbles to the TV without her walker and turns it on manually. Gregory Peck appears on the screen. Dee has forgotten John is on the phone, but he hears the TV and is comforted knowing that Dee will be up for a while.

A few minutes later:

CNA Rotty enters the room and wordlessly lays out Dee's pajamas. Methodically, Dee removes her slacks and places them in the drawer marked socks. She takes off her blouse, rolls it into a ball and places it in the drawer marked underpants and bras. She tries to slip on her pajamas but gets tangled. Rotty knows there is a care plan delineating instructions for each resident's care needs but she is already behind in her duties and reading takes time, so she just recalls that someone said Dee needs help brushing dentures in the am. and p.m. Rotty assumes the brushing was already done in the morning so she skips that step. Dee has her pjs on now, so Rotty lumbers toward the TV and turns it off.

Other CNAs have called her Dina Sore because she's been working there forever and often wails that her knees and feet hurt. She hates her job. She has threatened, "If they think I move too slow, they can just give me disability payments and I'll stay home." *But, no such offer is made.*

Now her left hip displaces weight from the right and the right hip displaces weight from the left as she plods through her shift and tries to hum along to the tune that Dee is mumbling, "Stayin' alive, ya, ya, ha, ha, stayin' alive... ."

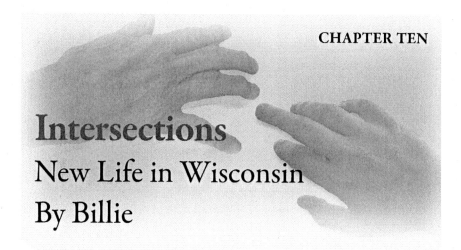

CHAPTER TEN

Intersections
New Life in Wisconsin
By Billie

−2003−

Mum still lives with me and my retired husband. Our retirement picture has changed somewhat, my mother being smack dab in the middle of it. We carefully anticipated our retirements and thought we were more prepared than most. I'm working one more year so I can retire with my full benefits. But we hadn't planned on a boarder, a widowed aging parent with a slowly progressing degenerative brain disease. And even if we had planned for that possibility, we would not have been prepared for its many ramifications.

Night time at our house—quite an adventure. Everything but a good night's sleep. Knocks on our bedroom door, Mum wanting to "go home," trying to fry an egg in the kitchen at 3 a.m., putting on her coat and mittens, grabbing her suitcase.

"Where are you going, Mum?"

"I don't know."

A thud. Mum has fallen again. Miraculously, no major injuries, but lots of X-rays.

The worst—panic attacks continued. Medication didn't completely control these. A sudden perception of being alone in the house might set off a panic attack. Then she would find the phone and call someone, just compulsive dialing. Breathless, too. Sometimes she couldn't stay in her bedroom at night, confused about where she was. She'd open my door. *Where is Ian?* But more frequently, *Where is my mother?*

She refused to go to respite care, day care for elderly with Alzheimer's. We were wearing out. When Mum first set foot in Wisconsin after what I call Operation Rescue, 2001-2002, people wanted to help. That was over a year ago. Visitor volume and reinforcements are dwindling now. Some friends and family have *moved on*. I had thought, prior to Mum's Alzheimer's diagnosis, moving on happened after a period of grieving following the death of a loved one. But Mum is very much still alive and experiences a full range of emotions. If she were a child and her father or mother moved on, that would be called abandonment. No one would condone it. It might be litigated, too. But for the unfortunate Alzheimer's victim, moving on can begin when the task of advocacy becomes inconvenient, unpleasant or gets, like the afflicted senior, old. The slow progression of this disease stretches and strains; it's an endurance marathon, and that is why the task of caretaking very commonly falls into the laps of a very few or even just one relative.

We didn't want to wait for a crisis we couldn't handle, so we looked into assisted living in the area: costs are staggering. No coverage by Medicare and no financial preparation on my mother's part.

Alzheimer's Association recommended a family meeting and everyone chipping in. I couldn't even get my relatives to chip in their time, much less thousands of dollars of their money. Most of my mother's English and Scottish relatives whom I barely know still lived in England and Scotland. I wished I'd had eight or nine financially independent and generous siblings, or maybe a kindly aunt with Oprah Winfrey's bank account. Ian claimed Mum had given him some money to invest for him. When we brought her to Wisconsin, he said he'd send us a check. I don't know if the amount was $40 or $40,000, but he didn't send the check, said he decided he had earned it taking care of Mum. The financial issues are bad enough, but there is more.

The inevitable crisis came. My cousin Margaret had come for a visit and left a bottle of aspirin in a drawer of the guest bathroom. Mum probably thought she had a headache or one of her *funny feelings*, must have come across that aspirin during one of her wanderings. I discovered the bottle in her room.

"Where did this aspirin come from, Mum?"

"I don't know. Isn't it yours?"

"Did you take some?"

"I don't know."

She used to take aspirin by the handfuls, she once confessed. I think this time she probably ingested a whole lot more.

That night she knocked on my bedroom door. Whenever I hear that knock, I bolt upright. My skin tingles. Then I get up and open the door. Feels like peeking into a nightmare. This time, "What's the matter, Mum?"

"It's hard to explain." Breathless. The breathless part is anxiety. She said something about the toilet.

I helped her shuffle back to her bathroom and looked into the toilet bowl. Full of blood. I gulped back a scream. My husband and I drove her to a hospital. There, her heart stopped beating twice. Doctors suspected heart disease and considered a pacemaker. But consultations with more doctors at a medical college determined that Mum was in hematologic shock. They sent her by ambulance to a bigger hospital. There she continued to bleed for six days. The head of surgery told us that six days is their gold standard; if they can't stop internal bleeding by that time, they have to do something. In Mum's case, it was remove the entire colon. He warned us that my mother's physical condition and her age were factors not in her favor, but that this surgery would end her bleeding. Her small intestine would be attached to her rectum and she would not require a bag. She just wouldn't produce the fluffy brown stool the rest of us enjoy.

We gave permission for the surgery. What else could we do?

Surgeons marveled at her quick physical recovery. Not aware of her catheter and not particularly patient, she climbed out of her bed in intensive care to go to the bathroom. "Tough old bird" they called her. As she recuperated, my husband and I decided we couldn't do this anymore on our own. Mum's doctors concurred that she should never be left alone and that a nursing home would be an appropriate placement. My sister and I began a whirlwind tour of area nursing homes; Mum would be released from the hospital in three days. With the aid of a hospital social worker, we narrowed our list of possibilities to 8. We had to rule out some we would like to have seen. At $7,000-$10,000 per month, we knew Mum would run out of funds shortly, Medicaid would take over. But some highly rated homes have long waiting lists, especially those with scarce Medicaid beds. The situation is different for residents who can self pay and who give the home an endowment. The least depressing of our options was a place called Riversite.

Unlike some others, Riversite was clean, smelled good and had spacious and cheerful dining rooms. It didn't have a designated Alzheimer's wing, but we had seen some of those units in other homes and the advanced stage those patients were in was just too frightening. We thought Mum was higher functioning than that population. Riversite had its own pool of nurses from which to draw when short-ages of staff occurred, but it was a huge facility and some wings seemed chaotic as one shift ended and another began, confusion and noise as staff were given assignments. But still, it was the best of the eight alternatives and in the area where I live.

After Mum's hospital release, we took her to Riversite. Admission day. Forms, end-of-life decisions, medical power of attorney, all this legalese mumbo jumbo and in front of Mum although she was too confused to follow, I think. I met her roommate Jessie who didn't speak to us at all, just sat in a wheelchair. We asked the aide why she didn't already have a roommate; what had happened to her last room-mate. I was concerned about her personality. The aide said she was actually a very nice lady and that the roommate Blanche had died; Blanche and Jesse had gotten on pretty well, she told us. The woman seemed like a mute to me. But then, I was new at this. While the social worker gathered together the forms, I took in the spare, dorm-like room. It seemed familiar.

∽∾∽∾∽∾∽∾∽∾∽∾∽∾∽∾∽∾∽∾∽∾

There is an image of the nursing home as a kind of billeting of sedate and feeble elderly, not the same picture that a state institution

for the mentally deranged conjures up. Somewhere between the two exists the reality of a modern nursing home, and some scenarios involving senile elderly residents are not unlike those dramatized in the book/movie *One Flew Over the Cuckoo's Nest*.

I had visited a local medical complex many years ago, the section that houses the—what is correct now—emotionally challenged? My ski/social club converted to a choir during the holidays and sang Christmas carols at hospitals. My group entered a locked unit. One man wore a helmet to protect his head as he banged it against the wall. I said Merry Christmas to another man and he burst into tears. Someone on the staff tried to console him but he sobbed and sobbed. I tried again and said Merry Christmas to a woman and she responded, "Merry Christmas, you monkey's ass!" Another resident had to be stopped as he pushed a piano down the hall. I think he was trying to go with us but he wanted the piano, too.

✣✣✣✣✣✣✣✣✣✣✣✣✣✣✣✣✣✣✣✣✣

That admissions day, I had been in my mother's room just twenty minutes when I heard a man's voice in the hall, "George, get in that chair! Now you stay there!" Then I caught an obstructed view of a man pushing a wheelchair past the doorway. A few minutes later, "I told you to stay there! Don't get up, George!" And I thought *I wish George would just sit in that chair*. Then, same two legs and wheelchair going by in the other direction and same demands, "Stay in that chair, George!" Finally, I walked to the door and scanned the hallway.

There was no one in the wheelchair. The resident was walking his empty chair. Cuckoo's Nest.

✣✣✣✣✣✣✣✣✣✣✣✣✣✣✣✣✣✣✣✣✣

Mum would be assessed for a while. She would wear an alarm bracelet until it was established that she wouldn't wander off the unit. If she tried to exit her floor on an elevator, an alarm would sound. Those are safety precautions, protections for the institution as well as for the resident. I had more immediate concerns. Mum and I both wanted to know where and with whom Mum would eat her meals. Someone on the staff pointed out the table and the fact that she would be dining with a resident named Dee and another woman—condition unknown. The aide explained that there had been a man at the table for four. Dee's husband used to come daily, was quite a presence, she said, until recently. So it was three women now. I stayed with Mum through that first meal. Dee smiled once in a while and talked a little gibberish. The other woman had a scowl on her face and said nothing. Mum did eat her meal. I was offered a plate, but I don't think I was ever less interested in food. No appetite today.

Walking out of that place that day—that was the heaviest I've ever been, the lowest I've ever felt about a decision I made. My condition gave new meaning to the expression *wet noodle*. Wave after wave of guilt, self-flagellation, worry and fear. But I did keep my promise I'd be back the next day and I am there almost daily, usually five times a week, alternating with my sister.

And I do believe, now that I know the operations of a nursing home, a daily advocate is something all residents should have and most don't have, so it is my intention to keep up this pace as long as I can. Hope I stay alive.

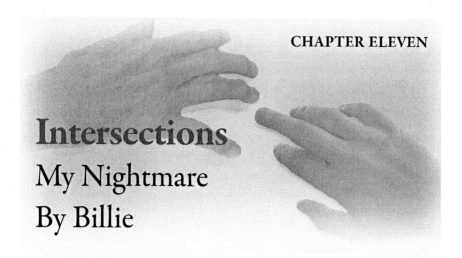

CHAPTER ELEVEN

Intersections
My Nightmare
By Billie

−2003−

Nearing the end of a long career teaching high school students, I have reached two conclusions. First, teaching high school students is a lot of things but it's never boring. There is no such thing as time that drags when you teach five classes a day, tutor in a writing center, run a study hall, and take paperwork home. The second conclusion is the difference between a job and a career. You punch out at the end of a "job" workday, and you check out psychologically. But, you take the "career" with you at the end of the workday, and you don't ever check out psychologically. Even in sleep, I have been visited by students. When my life is at a particularly chaotic point and I'm feeling a loss of control, I have the same dream:

I'm outside, in a forest, and need a toilet. I can't find a bathroom, but I do find a tent, sort of a teepee. I lift open the door flap. Inside I see a pit dug in the middle of the dirt floor. I remove my underpants and squat over the open hole. As my bowel movement ensues, I glance out the tent opening, horrified to see devilishly grinning faces of the five worst hell raising students I have ever had, gleefully catching me with my pants down.

I had that dream the night of the day I took Mum to Riversite. And when I wasn't dreaming, I was hearing sounds, like the knock on my bedroom door, kitchen noises, a thud, all the sounds I had become accustomed to in the night when Mum was here. I was literally hearing things. Feeling out of control. And I had to face my classes the next day.

Mum was admitted to Riversite on a Monday, so I took a day off of school. I was worried that my students harassed their substitute teacher. Actually, my sub hadn't had too bad a time. I didn't expect to fare as well. Sleep deprived, I expected to automatic-pilot-motor through the day, but not much more. Somehow, my students had been informed of the reason for my absence. One student stayed after class one period and told me she was sorry to hear I had to take my mother to a home. That was kind. Nice girl. But the day was young. By the last period, 8th hour, I'm starting to wear out even on a good day. And this wasn't a good day.

My life was easier when student John Nell just put his head down on his desk and fell asleep. That's what he sometimes did. When he was fully awake, which was seldom, his questions and comments were intended to subvert the lesson plan; he had an accomplice who was just slightly more aboveboard than he was, but the accomplice wasn't interested today. John Nell was a kid whose life had a lot of pain. He had been committed twice to an institution to dry out. Substances he abused included alcohol and illegal drugs. I don't believe he was ever completely sober or drug free except when he was in rehab. When he fell asleep in class, it wasn't because he was bored. It was because his body was ravaged by chemicals.

But the day after taking Mum to Riversite, he was wide awake and while I took attendance he blurted, "You took your mother to a home? How could you do that, put your mother away in a home?"

"Shut up, idiot," a girl muttered to him.

I felt completely vulnerable, like in the dream. I stared for a minute or two at my attendance card. Then I looked at John Nell. He was smiling, glee, the faces of the boys catching me with my pants down. He was smiling because he wanted to inflict pain and he found a way to do it.

"John, sometimes institutionalization is what a person needs. You should know that."

"What are you talking about? Rehab isn't the same thing and that's none of your business anyway."

Then he stomped out of the room. He wasn't upset; he had just orchestrated a way to cut class. If I reported him, he'd tell the principal that I told the whole class he'd been in rehab. I couldn't win, so I let it go. But the incident did, in fact, help my perspective. It is true—I heard myself say it—that institutionalization is sometimes what a person needs. Nursing homes like other intuitions, schools for example, aren't perfect, but they perform a service, fill a need. For Mum and for me and my sister and my husband, on May 21, 2003, the nursing home was the best we could do.

As for John Nell, he's been institutionalized again. He's 18, and he graduated to prison this time.

CHAPTER TWELVE

Rescues
On the Job
By Cate

−2003-2004−

C hristmas and a holiday weekend. Same thing that happened over Thanksgiving. One caregiver didn't show up; another called home, child sick. She said, "My child is my first priority." My frustration gave me unkind thoughts. *There are sick people here and when you took the job, you agreed to make them your priority.* Of course she had to care for her child, but her leaving meant my usual workload of ten residents would increase unless Riversite could come up with a last minute caregiver from the pool. Riversite didn't.

I know my sub-acute patients whom I am usually assigned, but the other wing is a mix of non acute custodial care residents. Like many others, they are here not because they are sick or need acute care but because they are disabled. They can't walk anymore; many suffered debilitating strokes prior to admittance, dementia sometimes, so their families/spouses, whomever they used to live with couldn't manage the care anymore. In some cases they lived alone; if you can't stand up, you can't take care of yourself. You can't get in and out of bed, on and off the toilet, or dress and undress.

So this afternoon I had my usual ten residents plus six more in my charge. Since some residents are physically unable to feed themselves, the dining hour can be a challenge. We grouped together the neediest residents to make best use of our reduced numbers. Unaware of the short-staffed situation, residents in the dining room seemed to enjoy our attentions, the Christmas music piped in, and the volunteer Santa Clause and elves from an area school providing entertainment. Disruption: An emergency alarm sounded from one of the rooms I was assigned. Addressing that alarm takes priority over feeding, so on my way, I asked a dining room aide to feed my patients while I tended to that alarm. She said, "I'm already doing residents that aren't mine." Everyone was edgy today.

The woman whose bed was armed with an alarm had recently gotten out of bed at 2 a.m., left her room without a walker and fallen in the hallway. Now, her walking, according to her care plan, should be with assistance only. The alarm was installed under her bed mattress. When she arises, it sounds inside her room, and loudly, so aides outside the room can hear it. The expectation is that a caregiver hears the alarm, immediately enters the room, checks on the safety of the resident, possibly preventing a fall, and turns off the alarm. Lydia had gotten up to turn on her television, no fall. And she was confused about the sound of the alarm in her room. Like most caregivers, I dislike this device. I've never known it to actually prevent a fall. It alarms the resident, the resident's roommate, and of course, it consumes a great deal of caregiver time if the resident is active.

After settling Lydia in her recliner, I left to return to the dining room, but a call light went on at the end of the wing. Residents who need assistance push a nurse call button and a light goes on in the hallway above the room. That light is a silent signal for nurse/caregiver assistance. Some residents turn them on incessantly, a room service sort of thing. Sometimes one patient is on a toilet pressing the call button while I'm in another room helping a patient who hadn't quite made it to her commode. Then I return to the first patient to help her back into her wheelchair. I get scolded for taking so long. Others are reluctant to use nurse call buttons at all; they don't want to bother anyone. Actually they just want independence, and they'd rather fall than ask for help. People problems are all part of my job. One of my therapist friends thinks I over perform in care giving to atone for what happened to my daughter. I don't know. I do know I like people challenges because I like people, helping them heal helps me heal. I need them as much as they need me. And many residents do appreciate my efforts, say so, and try not to demand more than I can give. I'm a fast worker, competent, and usually get all my work done by the end of a shift; even when I'm over assigned, I manage. Today was different.

The resident who used her call light at the end of the wing needed help toileting. She had no use of her lower body and very little strength in her arms, dead weight to lift. A mechanical lift should be used to avoid injury, but the contraption is time consuming without the assistance of another aide. Mechanical lifts frighten some residents, like my mom. The lifts are stored in the shower room and when she's taken in there she remarks, "It's the torture chamber...The Spanish Inquisition is here." Anyway, I could have told the woman to just wait, some caregivers do that, but this resident seemed distressed, so with considerable effort, I did get her on the toilet and told her I'd be back in a few minutes.

Meanwhile, from the public address system, *CNA Cate. Pick up the phone. You have a call.* There is a phone just outside Lydia's room. Lydia's alarm went off again. I dashed in to find her sitting on her bed wondering what all the noise was about. I turned off her alarm and returned to the hallway. Another call light had just gone on, and I hadn't answered the phone yet. The phone was closer than the call light so I picked it up.

It was Mom, calling from her wing. She sounded breathless, anxious. Told me she had on her coat and gloves and would I drive her home. *She should be in the dining room.* I tried coaching her into taking off her coat and gloves. *Were they short staffed on Jessie's unit, too?* I told her I was at work and would take her home to her mother later. "Oh, thank, you, thank you. What time?" I have had these high anxiety conversations with Mom before. Don't know what initiates the anxiety and semi-delusions. Her anxiety medication has been reduced. Lots of pressure from OSHA not to use *chemical restraints*. I think Mom needs them, though. Finally, I hung up and hustled to the room with the next lit call light. I passed the room where the first call light was lit again, where the woman was still on the toilet. "Help me, help me," she called. I hoped my stop in the second room would be only a minute. What a day.

In that second room, the resident lay on the floor, call light cord in her hand. She was unresponsive. I automatically initiated a code red.

❦❦❦❦❦❦❦❦❦❦❦❦❦❦❦❦❦❦❦❦

My supervisor was satisfied that I had followed protocol, that Riversite was not liable for injuries (which weren't serious) to the resident who fell out of bed. Actually, she applauded the fact that I had left the dining room over an alarm and a call light and that I had responded to a call light from a room that I hadn't even been assigned. Sally was a short term patient who was admitted to Riversite after her husband was hospitalized and couldn't care for her. Her blindness and related agitation, not negligence, caused the fall. She wanted to use the toilet, pressed her call button, and didn't wait for help.

What my supervisor didn't know was that I had taken a call from Jessie. She is a resident, but it was a personal call. I was no less guilty than the caregiver I criticized for ending her duty early. "My child is my first priority." The three-five minutes I chose to deal with Jessie rather than answer that call light were three-five minutes I could have been assisting Sally, three-five minutes that may have prevented her fall, three-five minutes *I wasn't there.*

After the episode, I privately examined my priorities, but my supervisor publicly designated me employee of the month.

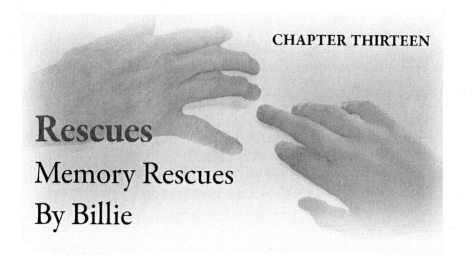

CHAPTER THIRTEEN

Rescues
Memory Rescues
By Billie

−2003-2004−

I interrupted Mum's television viewing one morning at Riversite. Comfortably seated in her recliner contentedly watching Gene Kelly dance, she declined a staff invitation to exercise class. I tried to persuade her to go.

"You'll never dance like Gene Kelly if you don't get some exercise, Mum"

"Okay, boss man."

After Mum's exercise class, an aide delivered her a.m. meds which now included folic acid and vitamin D, two supplements linked, recent studies showed, to improved memory. I'm keeping up with developments and Riversite has accommodated my requests. Next, I drove Mum to an American TV store because it provides special parking for seniors and use of a wheelchair. I asked Mum if she felt like the queen of the May as I pushed the chair and she said, "No, I feel like an invalid."

"Would you rather walk?"

"No," a cryptic response. Later she asked if I would like to sit while she pushed.

That all went well but repeatedly she asked, "Where are we going?" A change in geography increases her disorientation. We stopped for ice cream, right across the street from Riversite, but once reintroduced to the facility, more confusion. I noticed her lower lip trembling. Anxiety. Once inside, we couldn't pursue our usual routine - get a cup of coffee and return to Mum's room. A tornado drill was about to commence. I told Mum I used to have those in school. All the kids had to go out to the halls where they were safe from flying glass. Mum looked around and down the hall and asked, "Where are the teachers?" Yes, confused.

The drill seemed long and uncomfortable for some of the residents. A few could not be moved out of their rooms; staff pulled a drape around them. Several others didn't have a place to sit in the hall and standing for ten minutes demands more fitness than weakest of these residents have. Staff brought in chairs. Mum's walker has a seat, so she was physically comfortable, but her anxiety and impatience mounted so I retrieved a family scrapbook album from her room and used family history as deflection. I asked her if she remembered moving to Milwaukee. No, but she remembered Hodag. Okay.

"We lived at 216 Pelican Road in Hodag. Less than a block away a creek passed under the road through a concrete culvert. After heavy rains, dangerous currents forced water into the culvert leaving no pockets of air at the top. You'd have to hold your breath from one end to the other if you fell in. We kids used to play on the embankment and look for frogs. You and Dad warned us about not falling in. Well, here's an old newspaper article about probably one of the bigger events in Hodag history- a near drowning of guess who?

"Here it is: *Billie Roy, daughter of Mr. and Mrs. Lincoln A. Roy, 216 Pelican Road, nearly drowned Saturday. Billie was pulled from a creek by Donald Ackerman just before the current dragged her into the culvert under Flock Street. The creek drains Silt Lake and the swampland behind Haught Elementary School.*

According to police, Billie was tossing stones into the creek when she fell into the water. Riding by on his bicycle, Donald saw the girl in the water. He ran down the embankment, pulled the girl to safety, then went home to tell his mother.

The girl's father, a city patrolman, arrived on the scene and took his daughter to St. Anita's Hospital. She was released Sunday and is recovering at home from her experience.

Police had high praise for Donald. They complimented his quick thinking in rescuing the girl and in summoning adult help.

"Dad later proposed that the 'hero' on the bike who stopped to pull me out of the water after I'd emerged from the flooded culvert was actually the same boy who pushed me in. He didn't believe I just fell in. But even so, I wondered about the incident. Maybe Dad was paranoid? If the guy really did save me, doesn't he deserve at least a thank you? So I wrote to Donald's mother and asked for a way to contact her son because I wanted to thank him. She wrote back.

"Guess what she said, Mum."

"I don't know."

"She didn't mention her son. She said she knew Laurence Roy was my uncle and that he was a widower now. She was a widow herself and she wanted me to set her up on a date with Laurence."

"What?"

"Yes, and I asked Laurence and he said 'no thanks.' And looks to me like maybe Dad was right."

⊰⊱⊰⊱⊰⊱⊰⊱⊰⊱⊰⊱⊰⊱⊰⊱⊰⊱⊰⊱⊰⊱

Mum's attention quickly shifted to geography. "Why are we here?" she asked and the drill wasn't over, so yet another rescue story to rescue Mum:

"After Dad left the police force to become a meatcutter for higher pay, we moved from Hodag to Milwaukee's south side, 6th Street, I think. This was Polish town at the time, and I liked it there because we were close to my favorite relative, Aunt Craze, and Mitchell Street. Anne and Jimmy and I could walk to the Mojeska movie theater, pay a quarter and stay all afternoon. I liked to watch movies, especially animated ones, over and over. Westerns were good too, but I could get those on TV. Sometimes you, Mum, had to come to the theater and physically retrieve me and Anne and Jimmy."

"I don't remember that."

"A cranky old woman owned the flat and occupied the lower unit. She gave us dirty looks when we played in her back yard. I think she even banished us, can't remember why. So we played in the alley with some of the other kids or in other kids' little city yards. Having come from small town USA, Hodag, I had a more unsophisticated view of reality than did my new 'city' friends. I enjoyed 8-year-old drama of my own creation, so one day I suggested, 'Let's all lie down and play dead and see if the kids riding by on bikes stop to save us.' I thought they would stop to inspect the scene because that is what I'd do. My savvier neighbor friends did lie down but got up as soon as they saw boys on bikes cruising toward us. I remained, eyes closed, doing a fine acting job of dead—I thought dead people closed their eyes—when the bikers rolled right over me. I was beginning to learn *mean people*.

"There were bully types on the playground at school that I had to avoid, too. Once a boy threatened to punch me in the stomach. I said, 'You wouldn't dare!' So he punched me."

"I don't remember that! I'm sure I'd remember that!"

"Back on our block on the south side, there was a conspicuously solitary and odd older boy, maybe young man, who used to stand near-by and watch the young girls. If he were a brother or uncle or some-thing of one of my friends, that would have seemed just friendly. But he was a stalker. I avoided him. And one day, about the time I ordinar-ily returned home for dinner, I walked out of a friend's backyard past a second story porch. I saw the man hiding underneath. He grabbed me and told me not to scream. He put my hand on his penis and he said, 'What do you think that is?'"

"I said, 'It's a hot dog,' because that's what I wanted it to be. An ordinary, inoffensive Oscar Myer wiener."

I thought Mum might laugh as I told her that part, but she was too mesmerized, maybe abhorrent. Just stared at me. I'm sure her nau-sea had disappeared by this time, though.

"He said, 'Now let me feel yours.'"

"I screamed and cried and broke away. Actually he let me go because the screaming scared him. I highly recommend screaming. I ran home and of course you and Dad wanted to know what all the crying was about. I told every detail that I could recall, but I didn't know the man's name. The next morning, Dad said he wanted me to play in the alley and that he was going to be standing next to me until the guy appeared and then I was to identify him. Dad's sentinel duty lasted for hours. When he wasn't scanning the horizon for signs of the offender, he was watching my friends and I build imaginary teepees and shoot imaginary guns and become imaginary cowboys and Indians. I wondered if my assailant would have the nerve to appear in broad daylight. Meanwhile I was Sheriff Matt Dillon and sometimes I was Poncho, Cisco the Kid's sidekick, and occasionally Kitty who owned the saloon. We sang lyrics from television westerns like *Have Gun, Will Travel*.... 'Paladin, Paladin, far, far from hoooaaame , Paladin, Paladin, wheeerreee do you roooaaam?' and *Wyatt Earp*..., 'Wyatt Earp, Wyatt Earp, brave, courageous and bold! Long live his fame and long live his glory and long may his story be told.' And Johnny Yuma. He was a blond and blue-eyed Southern soldier, kind of a Swede in the desert... 'Johnny Yuma was a rebel; he roamed through the West...he got fightin' mad this rebel lad...he was leather tough and trigger at the hip when pushed enough, Johnny Yuma.' And always the good guy won. Finally my real life assailant appeared at the end of the alley. He was washing a car.

"Dad said, 'Is that the guy?'

"'I think so,' but I was second guessing myself, afraid he wasn't the guy and he would be punished for something he didn't do, a good guy mistaken for a bad guy. Dad looked glum. This was a Sunday morning, his day off, and he was spending it standing in an ally. Was he fightin' mad, my rebel dad? Probably. 'I think so, but I'm not positive, Dad.'

This wasn't pretend cowboys and Indians; it was real.

"Dad left his post and headed toward the suspect. I saw him speak briefly to the guy and then the two of them disappeared. It seemed they were gone a long time. I'm glad Dad was unarmed. When he came back, he was alone.

"'What happened to the guy, Dad?'

"'Oh, his mother gave him a spanking. He won't bother you again.'

"I was relieved, not so much because he wouldn't bother me again, but because he was the right guy, which is to say he was the bad guy."

∿∿∿∿∿∿∿∿∿∿∿∿∿∿∿∿∿∿∿

"You may not remember all this stuff, Mum."

"Well, I sure don't! You have a good memory!"

"How do you feel, Mum?"

"I feel fine; why do you ask?"

∿∿∿∿∿∿∿∿∿∿∿∿∿∿∿∿∿∿∿

"Years later, I asked Dad, 'What really happened to that guy?'

"'What guy?'

"'Wiener man. Frank Furter. P.D.File. Did you beat him up?'

"'Well,' with sigh that might betray regret, 'I did scare him pretty good. I took him home and there was just a mother, no dad. She was crying and he was crying. She begged me not to call the police. She promised they would move.'"

⧯⧯⧯⧯⧯⧯⧯⧯⧯⧯⧯⧯⧯⧯⧯⧯⧯⧯⧯⧯⧯

"I do think Dad beat him up, though, don't you, Mum?"

"He might have."

"I don't care if he did or not. I was only about 8. What mattered to me is somebody (Wyatt Earp, Cisco the Kid, Matt Dillon, Paladin, Johnny Yuma, Maverick, the Lone Ranger or Dad) came to the rescue. How differently might that episode have ended with no dad?

"And that's when we moved to Lake Foxbrook , and you finally bought me a pair of cowboy boots!"

"Boy, you have a good memory."

⧯⧯⧯⧯⧯⧯⧯⧯⧯⧯⧯⧯⧯⧯⧯⧯⧯⧯⧯⧯⧯

"Do you feel better, now, Mum?"

"Why, didn't I feel good?"

"You just needed a little rescue."

Actually, Mum needs a big rescue. A guy riding a big white horse, but black would do, a cowboy named Cure for Alzheimer's who would lift Mum into the saddle, ride off into the restorative sunset, then return her, totally Joan again.

CHAPTER FOURTEEN

Rescues
Cate's Fantasy Dream: Dead Women Walking

−2003-2004−

S cene: *Riversite, morning. Residents have assembled in their respective dining rooms. Dee, Jessie and Joan sit at the table in front of the fireplace. No one is talking and no one is smiling, but the space has an incandescent aura. The oak mantel of the fireplace seems more burnished than before. There is real heat coming from the unlit fireplace hearth. Unexpectedly, both CNA Cate and Joan's daughter Billie appear, right out of the fireplace flue, absolutely glowing, shimmering, other-worldly. Their movements are fluid; they float toward the table.*

Billie, *waving her liquid arms*: Cate, it's a miracle, what we found.

Cate, *so exited, she is confusing herself*: Billie, you can't imagine—I know you can't possibly, but of course you can—what this means.

Cate produces a small oblong pill from her watery fingers; she floats one to Jessie; then she produces another for Joan. Billie offers one to Dee. Joan, Jessie and Dee are momentarily mesmerized by the long, liquid fingers.

Cate: I am counting to three. When I say three, each of you put your new pill in your mouth. Okay. One, two, three. Now.

Joan and Jessie hesitantly put the pills inside their mouths and wait. Dee sets her pill on the table cloth and rolls it around with her fork.

Billie: Now you need to swallow your pills with water. *She touches Joan's mouth with her long aqueous finger, morphed now into a rivulet of water that flows into Joan's mouth. Cate does the same for Jessie. Dee stares, her mouth drops open. Just at that liquid moment, Cate pops a pill in Dee's mouth and directs the flow of water.*

Cate and Billie, *in unison*: "Now swallow."

All three swallow and at just that instant, the forms of Cate and Billie evaporate up the fireplace chimney before any Riversite staff has even seen them. In their wake is a tiny woman in a Broda chair.

Dee, Joan and Jessie sense a change. They are more aware of each other, drawn to each other. They smile among themselves. They recognize the little woman in the chair. An aide takes her to their table. She deposits coffee, cranberry juice, orange juice, oatmeal and toast. She checks the food menu for each resident and, satisfied that she got it right, moves to the next table.

Joan: "Dee, Dee. Can you hear me?"

Dee: "Of course I can hear you. What are you whispering for? You think I'm deaf?"

Jessie, *to Joan*: "Dee spoke complete sentences. And I think that's Blanche Dubois in the chair. "

Dee: "Well, how else would I speak?"

Joan, *to Blanche*: "I thought you died"

Blanche: "Nope. I'm staying alive."

Joan: "How do you feel?"

Jessie, Dee, Blanche, *in unison*: "Never felt better."

Dee: "So what are we doing here?"

Joan: "Well, I don't know, but I'm not staying."

Jessie: "You're going to leave?"

Dee: "Can I come?"

Joan: "They might try to stop us, but I don't think they know how fast we can move."

Dee: "Where will we go?"

Blanche: "Who cares? I know where I'm going if I stay here."

Joan: "Why do we need a destination? That's what this place is. I want the journey."

Jessie, *giggling*: "Oh, yes, to be in motion again. Oh, what fun, what fun."

Dee: Yeah. This time I'm going to enjoy the trip. So we're all in?"

Smiles all around the table.

Joan: "Let's get up from the table, bolt through the door marked emergency exit only."

Dee, *squealing her approval*: "Oooouuu. Okay. How far should we go?"

The four residents laugh. Two aides, eyebrows arched, look toward the table. Then they look at each other and grin. "Sweet but nuts," one mutters to the other.

Joan: "Let's just walk til there ain't no more tomorrow."

Dee: "I'm in. Count of three, let's roll."

Jessie: "Three!"

Suddenly, there are the sounds of bedlam. Dee, Joan, Jessie and Blanche's table is overturned, food flying through the air, the emergency exit alarm blaring, and four old women outside streaking alongside the river headed for the bridge, old lady cotton dresses billowing in front of them like filled sails. Before staff at Riversite even gets to the exit door, four senior sprites have made their crossing.

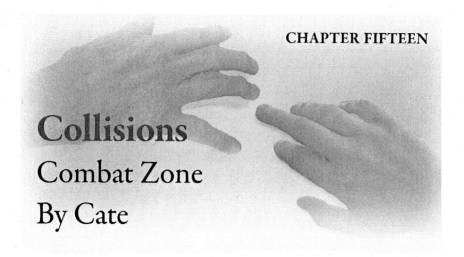

CHAPTER FIFTEEN

Collisions
Combat Zone
By Cate

—2004, Wisconsin—

I can have such good dreams. Wish there were more and that they came true. A happy pill I could give to residents. I mean, if we can't cure them, couldn't we at least keep them happy. Mom has settled into nursing home life. By that, I mean she's living from breakfast to lunch to dinner to bedtime. She's safe, can't hurt herself. Not happy, though. When Mom, who was widowed at the time, needed to move from assisted living to a nursing home, it wasn't my idea to put her in Riversite. I knew Riversite, strengths and weaknesses; I had been employed there before Mom came. Riversite wasn't a bad place. Like many nursing homes, staffing is big challenge. Nurse to resident ratios, for example. Some units have one caregiver per 12 residents, one RN per 30 residents. The numbers vary, and it seems there are never enough of us hired. My biggest reservation, though, was the absence of a designated dementia unit. The beauty of the designated unit is staff is generally better prepared, training wise, for the unique needs of Alzheimer's and other dementia afflicted people.

Mom wanted to be where I was; other family liked that, too, one of the family there, advocating, and Mom's needs then weren't as significant as they are now. Now, at Riversite, she still knows who I am, but staff seem like strangers to her. I sat on the bed in her room one day and an aide stood behind Mom, Mom seated in her recliner facing me. The aide wasn't smiling, but Mom didn't know that because her back was to her. Then the aide said, "Do you want some ice water?" Residents are kept hydrated, a good *thing*; an aide traverses the unit with a cooler of ice and refreshes the Styrofoam cups of each resident. But Mom hadn't understood what the aide said. She asked the question like she'd repeated it a thousand times, no longer enunciating clearly or slowly. My training taught me that Alzheimer's patients have trouble focusing, not trouble hearing. Sometimes they need a message repeated, not because it isn't loud enough, but because they can't process it all. The speaker needs to get in front of the resident, look at her, get her attention, then speak more slowly, not more loudly. Sometimes they process only the last couple of words. In this case, the aide stayed behind Mom and repeated, louder, "Do you want some ice water?" She didn't wait for an answer, picked up the cup, filled it and returned it, all from behind Mom who looked at me, confused. I am sure she did not know what had just transpired.

I joined Mom at her lunch table one afternoon. An aide approached her from the side. The aide set Mom's plate in front of her—a dry hamburger. Without establishing any eye contact, she said, "Ya wan maya?"

Mom said, "What?"

The aide repeated, "Ya wan maya?" Only louder. I couldn't stand it.

I said, "Mom, she wants to know if you'd like some mayonnaise on your hamburger."

Embarrassed, she apologized, "Oh, I'm sorry. No thank you."

These were days when I believed I'd made a mistake placing Mom here. But moving her to another facility now would be traumatic for her; Mom's biological children don't live nearby and since they are so relieved to have me involved in their mother's care, they never question my decisions on her behalf. I decided to make the best of a not-so-perfect situation and get involved in CNA training at Riversite. All staff are required to attend some in-services. The supervisor of nursing might support more training in dementia care.

Mom's care meeting was near; these meetings occur four times a year and I represent her family. Attendance isn't required, but I feel the same way about those as good parents feel about teacher conferences. I attend. My agenda would include some observations I'd made about weaknesses in dementia care at Riversite and some constructive suggestions about how to address them.

I had several scenarios to present. I started with this one. A new p.m. aide entered Mom's room, introduced herself and then asked, "What time do you go to bed?" Mom considered the question and in an appropriate attempt to avoid embarrassment, which she does feel, she said, "That is hard to say."

I took the caregiver aside. "She has Alzheimer's. She doesn't know what time anything is. She doesn't get time. That's why we have a care plan for you to look at. Did you look at it?" I know the aide didn't like my tone, I don't outrank her. She was flustered, defensive.

"I'm not usually on this wing," she muttered.

I framed these stories as a concerned family member of a resident would but I'm also a CNA, and my audience included the assistant director of nursing, an RN and the director of social services. The administrator listened without comment. I read disapproval on her face. I thought she disapproved of the caregiver I'd just described. The social worker seemed defensive. She said, "We can't be all things to all people." The RN said she could sympathize with my concerns, but was I aware that I had already alienated quite a few of the staff, that there had been several complaints about me? Did I know other caregivers did not like working with me? This wasn't the direction I expected the meeting to take.

I had been assigned to work on my wing with some veteran employees of Riversite, CNAs who had been there much longer than I. Two of them rarely had all their work done by the end of a shift. I hated to be assigned with them, had to take up their slack. So I reported them to my supervisor. Administration later questioned me. The CNAs in question avoided eye contact with me after that, continued not to cooperate when I asked for help toileting a resident, and continued avoiding resident requests for help if the request came close to the end of their shifts. Now, my integrity was in question. Had those two started some kind of a covert campaign against me? Or was I being paranoid? I was blunt again. "Those two are deadweight."

Then the administrator asked me questions that felt like interrogation. "Do you think your dissatisfaction with staff here has more to do with distress over the progression of your mother's dementia than it does with her care? Emotionally, you might be compromised. We do have some concerns about your sometimes intrusive involvement in Jessie's care, beyond what is healthful for the resident and for the resident's caregivers. And the fact that you've taken a combative tone with some caregivers concerns me, too."

Oh my God. They think I'm an emotional wreck. Am I?

So what did I do? I lost my temper and made their case. I shouted at a social worker, the RN, and an assistant director of nursing.

Now, I don't know what will happen because all has been revealed: I care about the residents, I love Mom, but I hate my job.

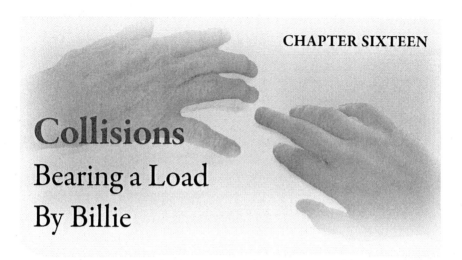

CHAPTER SIXTEEN

Collisions
Bearing a Load
By Billie

—2005—

C ate left Riversite. First, she tried to change her hours so she could go back to school and work part time. "Didn't work out," she said. Then, she quit working entirely and enrolled in a 4-year college program full time. She said an anonymous donor paid for tuition plus a living expenses stipend for four years, and she was going to be an RN, something Jessie had encouraged years ago.

"You think Jessie gave you the money?"

"No. I can't be sure where it came from, but it's money well invested, and a wise person, a *sophist*, would know that."

A benefactor like Sophia, I thought. Sophia from the Latin root sophista from the Greek *sophistes* meaning wise man.

So Cate and her daughter Christie are regular visitors to Jessie's dining room table about 5 p.m. most nights. Still, Cate says she's got problems with Jessie's family. Jessie never made her wishes for her old age maintenance known when she was fully able to express them. Now her two kids squabble over what needs to be done, especially now that Cate quit working at Riversite. Neither sibling wants to move here or have Jessie move there. Jessie's son wants to hire an advocate for Jessie, and he wants his sister to split the cost. The sister says things like, "She doesn't need a daily advocate. She doesn't even remember if someone's been there. She won't be worse for the wear." Those dismissals have long been familiar to me. There's a difference between visiting and advocating. Visiting is on Mother's Day...*how are you...and here are some flowers.* Advocating is any—every, ideally—day at any time. ...*How did she get those bruises on her wrist? Thank you for taking her to movie night. What did the podiatrist say about her foot? Why didn't she have dinner in the din-ing room? Thank you for putting clean linens on her bed.* Now Cate is con-flicted about Jessie, Riversite and Jessie's family and who knows what else, but at least she's on track for a future Jessie would applaud.

As for me, I thought I was doing all right. My husband is supportive. On the other hand, my sister and I have collided over daily advocacy. She's become a *won't be worse for the wear* apologist, too.

One way to deal with Alzheimer's to deny it. Either deny that a per-son has it; this tends to happen early on, or deny the victim's needs. A friend's mother suffering from Alzheimer's is in a nursing home. Her son and daughter-in-law are going to Florida to "winter."

"What about your mother?" I ask.

"Oh, she'll be fine. She's in a good facility."

Denial. Or maybe a conflicted relationship.

"She's in a skilled care facility. You talk like she's alone or something."

Denial. Or maybe guilt. If you ask a nursing home resident whether she feels "alone or something," she's not going to answer, "or something."

But the person in denial isn't as crass or cavalier as the remarks on the surface are. Denial can give a person a respite from pain. It's a coping mechanism, a survival thing. If you can't bear to think of your loved one in distress, deny the distress. Self delusional, but natural. Stressful for the primary caregiver, though.

My doctor discovered that my cholesterol is pretty high, plus my blood pressure has shot up this year. She asked me a lot of questions about my health, diet, exercise. And, "How is your mood?" That made me hesitate.

"It's okay," I said.

"What does *okay* mean?"

I don't know what it feels like to have a full fledged nervous breakdown, but I know what a mini breakdown is like because I had one right then. I couldn't even answer her question about *okay*, just opened my mouth and a loud sob came out. Then another and another. The doctor gave me a box of Kleenex, and I carried on like that for ten minutes before regaining enough composure to say, "I'm not okay."

Tranquilizers or antidepressants are an option, but the doctor suggested therapy. I did agree to join an Alzheimer's caregivers' group, but no one else in the group was the son or daughter of an Alzheimer's victim who is in a nursing home. They were all spouses of victims living at home. I was reluctant to share all I know about nursing home life. They were already in fear of that step. "It's the end, you know," one woman said. I thought, *that's not the worst part of it*. Then I didn't like myself for having that thought, didn't like the person I was becoming. There's the happy illusion that we have some *control* over our lives and that life will *comply*. Alzheimer's violates that trust. It's the rapist of happy endings. I liked myself more in the day when my mother knew who I was.

The group saw their needs as different from mine. One lady said, "I can't leave my house until someone comes over. At least you can get out." No empathy there for my situation. My mother is my new career; she's always with me. I'm a parent of a parent now. I can get away geographically, physically, but I never feel like I'm completely away from my mother. I can't disengage.

Except when Ian comes. I do get respite during his visits. He comes once or twice a year, rents a car, stays at a hotel, and for four or five days, dotes on Mum. I don't see either of them. Brash and bold, he can handle any situation that might arise at Riversite, I have no doubt. And although his history with me and with Mum is sullied with questionable financial practices and other women, there is plenty of evidence that in some way I just don't understand, after years of separation, Ian still does care about my mother. And all in spite of lately having heart health problems himself.

Hi Billie,

Sorry I have been lax but I've had problems health wise and spent extra time in Scotland for a second opinion ...

My blood pressure today was around 90/52 for several hours—I really don't know what's going on, that was a first.

Anyway I am coming up to Chicago on Monday evening, ... then will be picking your Mum up around 3 or four, maybe even two if things go well...

I have been—and am still—going through a lot of tests and proce-dures at the hospital which has made it awkward for getting up and I now see winter has arrived up there!!

... they are trying to find out why I get breathless at the littlest exertion.

But there are zillions a lot worse off than I am and I always think of your Mum and some of the poor souls in Riversite when I get a bit fed up.

Best Wishes,
Ian

If he succumbs to a fatal heart attack or stroke, I'm not sure how to handle that with Mum. Tell her that Ian died? I don't think so. For her sake, not mentioning Ian might be more kind. Lately, I show her a photo and she says, "He looks familiar." She's not clear some days who he is anyway. But his almost daily calls have a nurturing effect on her. After she hangs up, she forgets he called, but she feels good. Minus Ian, what would happen to that afterglow?

Before the visits, I remind him about Mum's inability to focus which makes her susceptible to falling, about the danger of mixing alco-hol with her medications and assorted other considerations. But he is in charge on the days he comes, spends many patient hours with her, and she says of those visits, "Oh, Ian and I always have a good time," although that is as much recall of events that she can summon up. Ian wrote a report:

She ... enjoyed just relaxing in the recliner in the room looking at old photos—she remembered the azaleas she'd planted around her Florida patio and her white Impala, but not the swimming pool or the neighbors. I was pleasantly surprised by her walking, on my arm and without a walker, but did notice more wobbliness.

And, yes, she went through a bag of gourmet decaf coffee plus a wee dram or two of brandy watered down but she giggled and expressed her delight at being the Queen, so it was a great four days.

I'd like to bottle Ian so whenever Mum is confused or bored or depressed or lonely, I could pour out just a little, enough to pep her up, but not enough to do harm. Then cork him!

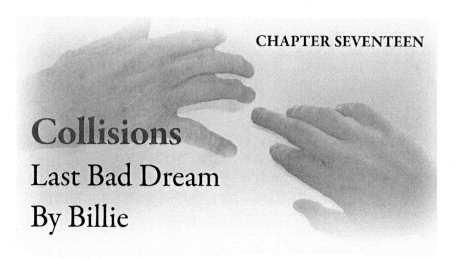

CHAPTER SEVENTEEN

Collisions
Last Bad Dream
By Billie

—2007—

Mum's mother and father never lived in America, but Mum often asks for them, especially her mother. *Where is my mother?* That is a most frequently asked question of Alzheimer's victims. A female resident of Riversite, someone from Mum's wing, fell down in the little lobby gift shop one Saturday afternoon. Paramedics preparing to take her to the hospital and staff there were genuinely distressed she couldn't be consoled, and no family member was there. The woman wanted her mother, just like soldiers dying on the field of battle or pilots in the seconds before the planes they are flying crash. They call out for their mothers. Mother must be the earliest comfort, the safest place. Mum's been insisting on contact with her mother for several years now. She thinks she should be home–Corby, England– at Christmas or should go home because her mother might be worried or wants to go home because she hasn't seen her mother in such a long time. She hasn't because her mother died 25 years ago.

The scene: *Ian is in town. The staff at Riversite marvel at the odd couple, younger man/older woman, wave to Joan and salute her with* *their cheer, "You go, girl!" Joan takes Ian's arm, and he whisks her out of Riverside and into his rental car. Ian and Joan glow in each other's company but, unfortunately, it is winter, cold and snowing. Joan hates the cold, so does Ian. Inclement weather adds more stress to his driving, and he is already worried about stress because of warnings from his doctor—his heart. But he hasn't seen Joan for months and she is happy, so they both let the joy of the moment carry them away.*

Ian pulls out of the parking lot and heads toward his hotel suite where the two of them can relax, and Ian can regale Joan with the events of his life. Joan will listen and appreciate the fact that she isn't asked to remember something. He asks her where she would like to go.

Joan: "I haven't seen my mother in a long time. Let's go visit her."

Ian doesn't want to tell Joan her mother died years ago, wants to keep things happy, so he begins to sing a song they both know, something from the past, from home, from Scotland. She does remember the Glasgow song, so they sing it together as Ian enters the freeway ramp.

Ian and Joan in unison:

"I belong to Glasgow,

Dear old Glasgow town;

But what's the matter wi' Glasgow,

For it's goin' roun' and roun'!

I'm only a common working chap,

As anyone here can see,

But when I get a couple o'drinks on a Saturday,

Glasgow belongs to me!

Chorus (Gaelic translated in brackets):

> Just a wee deoch an' doris [*last little farewell drink at the pub
> or celebration*]
>
> Just a wee drop, that's a' [*just a small drop, that's all*].
>
> Just a week deoch an' doris,
>
> Before we gang awa'[*before we go away*].
>
> There's a wee wifey waiting,
>
> And a wee bit in vain [*the little wife is waiting at home in   vain*]
>
> If you can say "It's a braw, bricht,
>
> Moonlicht nicht,

Well, you're a richt, d'ye ken!" [*But if you can say, "It's a lovely,
bright, moonlit night, then you are all right, d'you know," without slur-
ring, sober enough that is, to go home.*]

"It's a braw, bricht, moonlicht nicht, well, you're a richt, d'ye ken!"

*Then he clutches his chest with one hand, loses control of the car,
instinctively tries to protect Joan with the other hand. A retaining wall.
Impact.*

*Joan feels no pain. She has only a vague sensation of gentle floating,
floating above the wreckage where two motionless bodies lie. She is in
motion, traveling to a warm and bright light, irresistibly drawn, then
tugged back, then drawn again until the light forms a face. She wants to
go there, but something is pulling her back. Finally, Joan reaches, touches
the face and whispers her last earthly word.*

Joan: "Mummy."

CHAPTER EIGHTEEN

Collisions
Good Morning and Good Night
By Billie

—2007—

When I see Mum today, I will tell her.

You go, girl.

Special Thanks

Special thanks to the good folks who comprise the caretaker communities that nurture our aging parents: from the housekeepers and custodians to the doctors and nurses to the aides and CNAs to the administrators, volunteers and advocates. For the elderly that we place in your trust, your smiles are golden.

Inquiries by e-mail: ammsa@aol.com

Order additional copies:

$14.95 plus s/h $2.50

Check or money order to:
Caroline Court
P.O. Box 2619
Milwaukee, WI 53226-0191